HIS *Love* LESSON

NICKI NIGHT

HARLEQUIN® KIMANI™ ROMANCE

Recycling programs
for this product may
not exist in your area.

ISBN-13: 978-0-373-86452-2

His Love Lesson

H HARLEQUIN®
™ www.Harlequin.com

Printed in U.S.A.

"Is this how you ~~imagined your~~ ~~r~~ solo vacation would turn out?"

"Not at all."

"Me neither." Hunter sniffed out a chuckle. "This is actually better than I thought it would be."

Chey craned her neck, tossing Hunter a baffled look.

"I never thought I'd end up with a beautiful woman in my arms as we sat in front of a fireplace with a view of mountains beckoning at my side."

Chey's cheeks burned. She turned back toward the fire and let her head settle in the center of Hunter's chest. No words were necessary. Hunter was right. Despite all that had gone wrong, she could have never called this and was grateful that she didn't have to endure this alone. What would she have done had Hunter made his flight home on the first day?

"You smell amazing." Hunter's voice had reduced to a husky whisper.

"Thank you." Chey smiled but didn't turn around. "It's one of my creations." If Hunter kept it up, they would no longer need the fireplace for heat.

"You made that?"

"Yep."

"That's some talent." She felt Hunter nod.

"You

"Th

As t ~~he~~ ~~Hu~~nter insti ~~s enough~~
to k

Dear Reader,

I'm so very excited to share with you the second novel in the Barrington Brothers series, *His Love Lesson*. On this journey you will meet Chey Rodgers, a woman who is ready to take life on in a brand-new way. But the last thing she ever expected was for her plans to be intercepted by Hunter, the oldest of the Barrington brothers.

Chey Rodgers has put the past behind her and looks forward to a much brighter future—one where she finally puts her desires first. Her mind is on her career, not a relationship—until she crosses paths with Hunter. Chey may not think she's ready to let another man into her life, but for some reason, she can't keep her mind off Hunter. When they finally connect it's explosive, but then people and circumstances force them apart. Will they be able find their way back to each other? Together they will learn a valuable lesson in love.

Find out how Hunter finds his way back to Chey. I truly hope you enjoy their journey.

Happy reading!

Nicki Night

Nicki Night is an edgy hopeless romantic who enjoys creating stories of love and new possibilities. Nicki has a penchant for adventure and is currently working on penning her next romantic escapade. Nicki resides in the city dreams are made of, but occasionally travels to her treasured seaside hideaway to write in seclusion. She enjoys hearing from readers and can be contacted on Facebook, through her website at nickinight.com, or via email at NickiNightwrites@gmail.com.

Books by Nicki Night

Harlequin Kimani Romance

Her Chance at Love
His Love Lesson

Visit the Author Profile page at
Harlequin.com for more titles.

This book is dedicated to Benny Daniel,
my hero and the man who taught me how to go after
what I want without fear! Enjoy heaven, Dad!

Acknowledgments

Well, here I am again. First and foremost,
I must thank God for the doors that He's opened.
He gets all the glory for everything I've ever accomplished.

I'm excited to deliver my second romance novel to the
world, which wouldn't have been possible without many
great, wonderful and brilliant people! To all the readers of
Her Chance at Love, thank you for giving me a chance.
To my editor and the entire team at Harlequin.
Glenda Howard and Shannon Criss,
thanks for all you do. To my literary sisters, Zuri Day,
Donna Hill, Brenda Jackson, Beverly Jenkins,
Victoria Christopher Murray and
ReShonda Tate Billingsley, thanks for your ears,
advice, time and friendship.

To the best support system in the world,
the love of my life, Les, the Daniels Clan and my
entire family, thank you for always being there for me.
To my girls, for keeping me inspired, laughing and
for buying every book, I love you all dearly.

#DreamEnormously darlings!

Ciao,

Nicki

Chapter 1

"Is this the runaway bride?"

"Runaway fiancée! Get it right. We weren't married yet," Chey Rodgers said, snickering at her witty response to her sister's greeting. Deanna was obviously amused. Chey cut into her fit of giggles. "How's Mom and Dad, silly?" she said as she folded her legs under her bottom on the loveseat in her tiny living room.

"Dad is Dad. Mom is…Mom. Same snarky old woman!" Deanna laughed but stopped abruptly. "Don't tell her I said that." She laughed again. Chey shook her head and smiled. Her sister always managed to lighten her mood.

"I called her, but she didn't answer." Sometimes it was a relief when her mother didn't answer. They were still at odds about Chey's move.

"She's probably out with the church ladies."

Chey looked at the date on her laptop screen next to her on the loveseat. "You're right. It's Thursday. I'll call her in the morning."

"You know she's still upset about everything that happened. She can't seem to understand why you broke off the engagement and ran off to New York so quickly, or 'that big ole city,' as she puts it."

"Deanna, I've tried to explain that to her so many times. You guys don't know the Todd that I know. I couldn't attach myself to him till death did us part." Chey twisted her lips, mocking the twisted way people chose to see her big move. "I've been planning to go back to school for so long. I know this whole thing seems scary to Mom, but this was my chance and New York is where I need to be for what I want to do."

"So…" Deanna paused. "How's the big city treating you?" she said.

"New York has been great so far."

"Have you heard from him yet?" Deanna asked cautiously.

"No." *Thank God.*

"I'm surprised. You left months ago." She seemed disappointed.

"Our relationship was over way before it was officially over. He's so self-absorbed. He probably thinks he's punishing me by staying away." Chey rolled her eyes as she thought about her manipulative ex-fiancé. She hadn't called to talk about Todd Coleman. He had finally been relocated to his rightful place in her life—the past. "I cut my hair." She changed the subject and instinctively ran her fingers through her short crop.

"Really!" Deanna squealed. "I can't believe it. How much did you cut?"

"All of it."

"Uh! Excuse me?"

"I got one of those pixie cuts."

"Oh my goodness, Chey! I have to see it. Send me a picture."

"I will. Oh! And I can't wait to start school." Chey scrunched her shoulders in excitement.

"When do your classes begin?"

"End of January. I'm taking a little vacation to celebrate before I start."

"Wow. I can't imagine going back to writing papers and attending classes again. You've wanted to do this for so long."

"I know, but what could I do? We simply ran out of money and since the shop wasn't doing well, Mom and Dad couldn't help. It was almost depressing, seeing my classmates graduate without me. Once the shop started doing better, I could finally afford to save enough to go back."

"We have you to thank for that! It will all work out. You deserve this. Good luck! Where are you going for vacation?"

"Near Salt Lake City, Utah."

Chey pulled the phone away from her ear when her sister screamed, "What the hell is in Utah?"

"I booked an amazing villa. I plan to ski, snowboard, drink hot chocolate in front of a cozy fire and work on that book that I've wanted to write forever."

"I'm going to have to report this identity theft because you're clearly not my sister."

"This is just the beginning," Chey declared.

"I love it! I may need to take a page from your book. I could use some excitement. Maybe I'll come for a visit. You know how much New York City intrigues me."

"Great idea! Let's put it on the calendar."

"It's a plan!" Deanna gasped. "But I'll wait until your spring break. That cold weather is unbearable. Anyway, I gotta run, sis! I just realized I'm late for a conference call. You know how it is dealing with coworkers on the West Coast. The time difference is a killer. Give me a call tomorrow. Okay? Love ya." Deanna ended the call before Chey could say goodbye.

Since Deanna was a data analyst who worked from home, she was always mindful of making sure her bosses knew that she was a diligent employee. Even though she often worked from their parents' variety shop, she was sure to get her reports in and respond to emails or calls as quickly as possible so her bosses would never have to question her dedication or whereabouts. She needed this job, since the family business didn't pay much at all.

Chey laid the phone on the side table closest to the love-seat and walked over to the mirror near the door. Twisting her head, she took in the sleek look of her new hairstyle and ran her fingers through it once again. She recalled how nervous she'd felt when she'd sat in the hairdresser's chair with a picture of Halle Berry and told her she wanted to look like that.

When the stylist finished, she'd been shocked at how different she looked. At first she'd wondered if her sudden change had been too drastic. In the days following, Chey would absentmindedly attempt to run her fingers through her hair and be reminded that she had chopped all of it off. As the days passed, Chey had received loads of compliments at her part-time job and eventually became so pleased with the style that she wondered why she hadn't cut it before. Her new look highlighted her high cheekbones and made her big brown eyes pop in a good way. Then she remembered. She'd kept it long because Todd preferred that length.

Feeling free and light was becoming addictive. Chey had taken other actions and made plans to do things she had wanted to do for years. Now that she was no longer tied to Todd, she did whatever she desired and it felt great!

Chey's phone rang. She walked over to retrieve her cell

from the side table. She didn't recognize the number but did recognize the area code as being from her hometown in Virginia. It had to be someone she knew.

"Hello," she said in the same courteous tone she used at work.

"Chey?" Todd's greeting sounded more like a scolding.

Chey hadn't heard from him since the day she left home three months before. She resisted the initial urge to hang up. There was no reason to hide from him.

"Hello, Todd." She kept her tone professional.

"I've given you enough time to get over whatever little fit you've been having. It's time for you to come home. I need you here."

Chey found herself laughing at how ridiculous he sounded. "You can't be serious."

"You find this funny?" He was clearly annoyed.

"As a matter of fact, I do. It's not that at all, is it? You don't like the idea of me being independent. You can't handle the fact that I walked away from you! This is a joke!"

"This has gone on long enough."

Chey dropped her head into her free hand and shook it. "Todd. We're done. I have a new life. I truly wish you the best with yours."

"Tell me where you are."

"Goodbye, Todd." Chey ended the call, but not before hearing him declare that he would find her.

Chey walked to the refrigerator and pulled out the bottle of champagne she'd purchased to bring in the New Year. Suddenly she felt as if there was no need to wait the few days. She popped open the bottle and toasted to all the fresh starts of the past few months and the ones on the horizon.

Chapter 2

Hunter looked across the roomful of people at his brother Blake snuggled up against his fiancée, Cadence, on the couch and wondered if settling down was somewhere in his future. No one ever anticipated Blake finding a wife before his big brother, Hunter, who was more laid-back. Drew, forget about it! As the youngest, he was the rebel, completely commitment phobic and having way too much fun running through as many women in as many countries as he possibly could. Jade Donnelly, the only woman the family thought could have been "the one" for Drew, had run off with a chunk of his heart and was never to be seen again. Hunter believed that there was a slight possibility that Drew might have been holding out for her return.

"Hey, bro. You don't hear me talking to you." Drew pulled Hunter from his thoughts, bringing him back to the roomful of music and people attending his brother's New Year's Eve party.

"What's up?" he asked, sipping the champagne in his hand.

"I said, look at Blake—he's a sucker for love." Drew's

infectious laugh roared, garnering the attention of nearby guests.

"Yeah! Rightfully so, though. Cadence is a great catch."

"You're right. I'm just teasing. She's good people!" Drew took a long swig of his beer. "What about you? You think you'll find someone that would make you want to quit the singles game?"

"I don't know, li'l bro. I don't know." Hunter sipped again.

For a moment, Drew seemed caught in pensive thoughts. "I don't know either."

"What about Alana? The two of you went out before, right?"

For a quick second, Drew looked uncomfortable. "Hmm, Alana," he said with a puzzled expression. Hunter gave him a look that told him he wasn't buying his poor attempt at acting as though he didn't know whom he was talking about. "Oh! Pfft!" He waved his hand dismissively. "She's cool."

"Ha!" Hunter shook his head at him and continued sipping.

"Hey, Hunter!" said some girl dressed in baby pink, looking like a happy Easter egg.

"Hey…" He hesitated, trying to figure out if he knew her name.

"Tricia," she paused a moment, apparently waiting for some sign of recognition to spread across Hunter's face. "I recently joined the New York Association of Attorneys."

"Oh! Okay." Hunter had no idea who this woman was. "Nice to see you, Tricia." He held out his hand to shake hers. She was pretty enough not to forget. Hunter discreetly took in her curves. Obviously, he wasn't inconspicuous enough. She smiled seductively and arched her back slightly, giving him an unobstructed view of her ample cleavage.

"I guess I'll see you around," she said, then turned slowly and swayed her hips, leaving an imprint on Hunter's mind with her seductive gait.

"Who is that?" Drew reappeared by his side, ogling the woman as she walked away.

"Tricia!"

"Tricia?"

"Yeah…Tricia," Hunter said, still eyeing her. Though she was beautiful, he already knew she wasn't "the one" kind of material.

Hunter shook his head hard. Why was he even thinking like that? He hadn't been assessing the women he met in order to determine if any of them might be "the one" material before. Maybe he was just caught up in all the love oozing from Blake and Cadence.

Hunter looked over at Drew, who was still taking Tricia in, and laughed. He was at a New Year's Eve party. It was time to act like it. Old-school R & B floated through the hidden speakers. People were bunched in groups, chatting, laughing and sipping everything from hard liquor to bottles of water.

"Hey, Blake!" he yelled, snaking through the lively crowd with his empty flute leading the way. "It's almost midnight! We need to get more champagne in here."

Hunter's announcement caused a stir of cheer. Excitement rose in the atmosphere.

Blake gave Cadence a quick peck, which brought a sweet smile to her face, and then jumped up. "Let's get some more bottles from the cellar."

"Turn on the TV!" Alana, Cadence's best friend, shouted. "We have to watch the ball drop!"

Hunter and Drew accompanied Blake to his basement

to retrieve more chilled bottles of champagne. When they returned, the crowd made a show of cheering them on as they carefully balanced several bottles in their arms on their way to the table reserved for beverages. Blake danced to the music as he opened a few of the bottles.

The party flowed on, getting louder as it drew closer to midnight. Hunter caught Tricia watching him from across the room. Nodding, he acknowledged her but kept his distance—surprising himself. Any other time, he would have had a pretty girl like that eating from his skillful hands, enjoying flirtatious chatter as he competently weakened her resolve—if in fact there was any resolve to weaken. Hunter simply smiled and raised his glass to her.

Despite the frenzy surrounding him, Hunter retreated into his own thoughts. He'd caught Tricia's continued glances. Her seductive smile was stamped on his mind's eye. Being a man who was keen on women's behavior, he summed her up in seconds. Though she was beautiful, she seemed a little too eager. Like many men, Hunter loved the chase. He didn't mind putting in a little work to earn a woman's affection. The challenge was intoxicating.

"Thirty seconds!" With her champagne glass held high, Cadence yelled, "It's almost time!"

Hunter became aware of his surroundings once again, taking in the excited voices and the clamor of the guests gathering in front of Blake's TV. On the large flat-screen, the camera panned across the thick crowd of people in Times Square before cutting to the crystal-encrusted ball. The ticker on the TV indicated that there were only twenty seconds left in the year. Blake made his way to Cadence's side. The sight of Drew being so close to Alana wasn't lost on Hunter. He felt Tricia's eyes on him from across the room. Everyone joined the countdown for the last ten seconds. As they drew closer to the final moments left in the year, excitement crackled in the air like fireworks.

"Five! Four! Three! Two! One! Happy New Year!" they all shouted in unison.

Glasses lifted in the air before sips and swallows drained them dry. Blake had taken Cadence in his arms. They kissed as if no one else were in the room. When Drew hugged Alana, it lingered. Lovers became entranced in deep long lip-locks. Others shared hearty hugs and friendly pecks. Hunter gave his brothers, cousins and a few male friends high fives.

After pulling back from his cousin Lance Barrington, he noticed Tricia had slid across the room and was now standing at his side. Mischief sparkled in her eyes as she raised her glass and said "Happy New Year" before wrapping her pink-painted lips around the rim of her champagne glass. Hunter felt as though a match had been lit somewhere in his loins. Tilting his glass, he too took a sip, never breaking eye contact.

Hunter licked his lips and winked. A smile exploded across Tricia's face.

"Don't I get a hug?" she asked seductively.

"You can have more than that," Hunter leaned forward to kiss Tricia on her cheek. Just before his lips landed, she turned, surprising him with her plump lips. Hunter wasn't one to shy away from a challenge and in response gently parted his mouth. She received his tongue zealously.

Hunter knew right then that she would end up in his bed, but he also knew that she definitely wasn't "the one."

Chapter 3

The week had gone by in a flash and despite Hunter's attempt to be prepared for his annual trip with his frat brothers, he found himself doing a lot of last-minute running around before hitting the road.

"Mom! Dad!" he called out as he entered his parents' home in Long Island through the garage entrance.

"I'm in here, baby!" Joyce, his mother, called out from their laundry room.

Hunter followed the sound of her voice. "Hey, Ma!"

"Hey, honey!" Joyce reached up on her toes to give her eldest son a hug and kiss. "Are you all ready for your trip?" Joyce turned back to the clothes she'd just washed. "I don't see why you need to go all the way to Utah when we've got enough snow right here in New York," she said, snapping the towel she'd just pulled from the dryer.

Hunter laughed. "You know we try to go to different resorts every year. This will be our first time in Utah. Everyone is pretty excited about it."

"Well, I guess that's good, then. Your dad hasn't gotten back from the gym yet."

"Why didn't you go with him?"

Joyce stopped what she was doing and looked at Hunter with twisted lips. "Your daddy bugs me when we go to the gym together. I have to do things at my pace. At my age, I'm not trying to be Serena Williams. Daddy doesn't understand that, so we go to the gym separately."

"Ha! Dad is still pretty competitive."

"Yes, he is! Now, what time are you leaving?"

"Six in the morning. I have a few more errands to do, but I wanted to see you and Dad before I left."

"Have you eaten breakfast yet?"

"Just a cup of coffee."

Joyce folded the last towel and set it neatly on top of the others. "If you have time, let me make you a quick breakfast and he should be here by the time you finish eating."

Hunter couldn't say no to spending time with his mother. "Can you make me an egg sandwich?"

"That's all you want?"

"Ma! You make the best egg sandwiches." Hunter's smile nearly split his face in half. "Nobody prepares them like you."

Joyce shook her head and carried the laundry basket with her to the kitchen with Hunter on her heels. She washed her hands and then somehow guided the conversation in the direction of Hunter still being single.

"How are you going to let Blake get married before you? Do you even want to get married? I don't know about you young people these days. Everyone wants to stay single. What kind of life is that? You need someone to rock on the porch with when you get old." Joyce propped her hands on her hips.

"I didn't say I don't want to get married. I just haven't found the right woman."

"Are you even looking?" Joyce frowned, then turned her attention to the frying pan on the stove.

Hunter cleared his throat and then heard the churn of the garage door. He was saved! Jumping up, he headed for the door leading to the garage to greet his father as he pulled in.

"Hey, Dad!"

"Hey, boy! What brings you by?"

"I leave for my trip tomorrow. I just came by to see you guys before I left."

"Oh, yeah! Tell the fellows I said hello."

"Will do!"

Floyd stepped in carefully and walked over to Joyce in their sizable kitchen with a limp. Joyce inclined her head toward her tall husband. Floyd kissed her forehead. Something that all the towering Barrington men did with her.

"What happened to you?" She looked down at his leg.

"I think I pulled a muscle at the gym."

She looked at Hunter with a look that said, *See what I mean?* Hunter chuckled.

"Go on and get your shower. I'll fix you something to eat."

"Thanks, babe!"

Hunter assumed that the interruption of his father's entrance was enough to shift the conversation. To his dismay, Joyce went right back to the same subject.

"Well? Are you looking?"

"No, Ma. I haven't exactly been looking, but I do think I'll know when the right one comes along."

Joyce placed Hunter's plate in front of him and poured a glass of orange juice for each of them. She took a sip and eyed Hunter. When he noticed how intently she was watching him, he stopped chewing and looked back at her curiously.

"Humph. I hope she comes along sometime soon. I'd

love to have a few grandchildren before I leave this world. I need granddaughters to leave my jewelry to."

Hunter chuckled and began eating again.

"So, the woman you left Blake's house with on New Year's Eve apparently wasn't the right one?"

Hunter almost choked on the chunk of egg sandwich he'd just bitten. For a quick moment, he wondered how his mother knew, but he was sure it had to be Drew who'd opened his huge mouth. He was the youngest and had been the tattletale since they were kids. Only he told everyone's business except his own.

"Let me guess! You spoke to Drew?"

"Humph." Joyce didn't confirm or deny anything. "You're thirty-two now, honey. It's time to do what men do. Find a nice woman, have a family and take care of them just like your dad did. Trust me. You don't want to grow old alone."

Hunter quickly finished his sandwich so he could make a clean exit. He thanked his mother and ran upstairs to chat with his father before leaving. As he walked out the door, Joyce called out to him.

"Don't forget. You're a Barrington, son. Don't waste too much time with women who aren't well intentioned enough to bear your last name. The Barringtons worked some of the biggest, most important cases in our African-American history. You know they wanted your dad to run for office, but he refused—said he didn't do politics."

"Yes, ma'am!" Hunter stood erect and saluted his mother. He'd heard the stories all of his life. Of course he was proud of his family's legacy.

Joyce tossed the cloth she was using to clean the counter at him. He caught it, carried it back to her and pulled her into a tight hug.

"See you when I get back, lady," he said and bent over to kiss her on her forehead.

Hunter jumped into his SUV, revved the engine and pulled out of his parents' wide driveway. Down the road his phone rang. He answered the call through the car's Bluetooth system.

"Hey there, cutie." Tricia's seductive voice warmed the inside of the vehicle.

"Hey, yourself."

"Are you ready for your trip?"

"Almost. I still have a few errands to run."

"Want me to come over tonight and help you finish packing? I'll make it worth your while."

Joyce's words came crashing into his thoughts. *Don't waste too much time with women who aren't well intentioned enough to bear your last name.* He couldn't say he didn't enjoy Tricia's company. Any man with the senses he'd been born with would enjoy a woman like her. Yet Hunter knew he wasn't interested in her for the long term and in that moment decided that he'd cut this thing short as soon as he got back from his trip. As for now, he'd try to find a way to politely let her down. Maybe.

"That would be nice, but with all that I have to do, I wouldn't even have the time to enjoy your company. My flight leaves at six in the morning, which means I have to get up and out of the house by no later than four fifteen, four thirty at the latest."

"I could stay the night."

"I'd hate to wake you that early and you have to go to work."

"I wouldn't mind. I doubt we'd be doing much sleeping anyway. I'll just down a five-hour energy drink to get me through the next day. I've done it before."

Hunter fell silent. When she said that she'd done it before, he wasn't sure if she was referring to downing the energy drink or staying up half the night with another man. He preferred not to ask.

"That didn't sound right, did it?" She laughed. He didn't laugh. "In any case. I'll be home early. Call me if you want me to come by. I'll be waiting," she crooned.

"Okay…" Hunter paused there, refusing to finish with the words at the edge of his tongue, *I will*. That was because he knew he wouldn't. "I'll call you when I get back so we can have dinner. How's that?"

"Bummer! I wanted to see you before you left." She groaned. "Enjoy your trip. I'll see you when you get back."

Hunter thought it impolite to end their rendezvous in any other way than in person and tonight he truly didn't have the time to deal with that. Besides, waiting until next week would give him time to come up with a mannerly way to let her know that despite the fun they had during the past week, he wasn't interested in pursuing a relationship with her. Those conversations never went well, and he didn't expect this one to be any better.

Chapter 4

With just a few days left before her trip, Chey could barely concentrate. There was so much to do, including going to her new school to pay the small remainder of tuition that was left after her partial scholarship, and getting her schedule. She couldn't remember a more exciting time in her life. She hadn't been this eager while planning the wedding that had never happened. Deep down, she knew that accepting Todd's ring had been a mistake. The last draw had been when he'd ordered her to stop wasting time "tinkering with those silly perfumes" that she used to make in her kitchen. Little did he know they were bestsellers at her parents' store and had saved them from having to close the shop's doors. Not only had the perfume sales pulled the shop's finances out of the red, but they'd allowed her to save enough money to move up north and finish her last semester so that she could finally obtain her bachelor's degree. Patrons had come into the shop all the time pining for her latest creations, loving the aromatic essence of her skin-care products and perfumes—and still did. Before leaving Virginia, she'd made a huge batch of the few varieties the customers liked the most so that her parents wouldn't run out of stock while she was in New York.

New York—the city where dreams came true! Chey twirled in her tiny one-bedroom apartment with her hands outstretched. She was looking forward to fulfilling her dream of finally getting her degree as a chemist and launching her career as a perfumer. This city was the perfect place for her profession. She fantasized about working for companies like Estelle London, designing fragrances and creating skin-care products, or even opening up her own cosmetics company.

Chey flopped down on her bed and lay back, thinking of all of the possibilities until her phone rang, interrupting her musings. Sitting up, she reached for the phone and when she recognized Todd's number, she sent it to voice mail and tossed the phone aside. Unfortunately, she couldn't get back to that pleasant state of mind, because Todd's call had taken her off course.

Chey got up to finish packing when she swore she heard someone calling her name. At first she ignored it. In the three months that she'd been in the city, she hadn't befriended many people. She folded a few thermal shirts to wear under her sweaters and placed them in her suitcase when she heard her name again. This time she was sure of it. What puzzled her most was that the voice sounded much like Todd's.

Chey ran to the window, looked down onto the street and balked. Moving back, she hoped he hadn't seen her. Todd called her again. How had he found her?

"I saw you, Chey. Now please, open the door."

Chey couldn't believe this was happening. Containing a sudden urge to scream, she balled up her fists and traipsed four flights down to the entrance. She wanted to leave him there but figured that ignoring him would cause a scene.

Chey swung the door open. Todd stood there looking foolish to her with a bouquet of flowers that had been purchased from the corner store at the end of her block. It was an obvious afterthought.

Holding the flowers out to her, he asked, "Can I come in already? It's freezing out here."

Chey rolled her eyes, snatched the flowers from his hand and turned around. Todd followed her up to her apartment. Once inside, Chey turned around and faced him with her arms across her chest.

"How did you find me?"

"It was easy." Todd scrunched his face, dismissing her question. "Your mother eventually told my mother. She was concerned." He clapped his hands. "Now let's talk about you coming on home." He spoke to her, but his eyes took in the small neat space around them. "This is where you're living?" he asked with an expression that resembled disgust.

"Yes, this is where I'm living, and no, I'm not coming home." Chey took a breath. She was going to have to speak to her mother—again! She'd asked her not to tell Todd that she'd moved to New York. No matter how many times she said it, she couldn't convince Mrs. Rodgers that Todd wasn't the right man for her. She had been concerned only with the fact that he would have been a great provider. Coming from humble means, Chey understood but wasn't willing to let her dreams die under Todd's misogynistic thumb.

Exasperated, Todd grunted. "Okay, what's this really about?" Chey couldn't believe his attitude. "I've given you time. You should be back in Virginia planning our wedding."

"Todd! There won't be a wedding!"

"What's gotten into you?" He looked genuinely confused.

"Sense! That's what!"

His face changed; his new look bordered anger. "You're saying being with me didn't make sense. I'm a prominent attorney. Need I remind you that I'm being promoted to partner? I come from a wealthy family. Certainly it makes more sense for you to be with me than any other man. Who else could offer the life I'm capable of providing for you?" His expression changed again as if he'd just put the pieces of a puzzle together. "That's it! There's another man." Todd stepped past her as if he would find him in the apartment. "Where is he?"

"Todd!" Chey dropped her head and groaned. "There's no other man!"

"So why did you run away?"

"Ugh! I don't want to marry you?"

"Why on earth not?" Todd was baffled.

"Because you don't respect me?"

Todd gave a dismissive wave. "Of course I do."

"No, you don't. I have no interest in being the kind of wife you're looking for."

"What's that supposed to mean?" Todd remained clearly confused.

"I want to work, make my own living. I have a dream to become a perfumer." Todd cut his eyes toward the ceiling. "See what I mean? That's my passion and I can't be with a man who wants to control every facet of my life and would never support my dreams."

"Your dream is silly! I mean, really. Who makes a living creating concoctions in the kitchen sink? My wife doesn't need to work. Your job would be to raise our kids. Wouldn't that be enough?"

Chey couldn't stand there another moment. How could

someone young have such a dated outlook on life? "Get out, Todd!"

He stared at her, not believing she had ordered him to leave.

"Playtime is over!" he bellowed. "This is becoming embarrassing. I'm tired of my family's questions about your whereabouts. This stops here." Todd looked around and walked toward the suitcase that Chey was packing for her trip. "You're going somewhere?"

"Yes!"

"Where?" He closed in on her, demanding an answer with his words and presence.

"That's none of your business." Chey crossed her arms, refusing to back down.

"You are my business!" He stomped. Chey stepped back and looked at him incredulously. Todd huffed. "See how angry you make me? Let's go. Now!"

"Todd! For the last time. I'm. Not. Leaving. Here!"

Todd looked as though he hadn't understood a word she'd said.

"Let me make this clear. We're through. I'm never going to marry you. I have legitimate desires and dreams. I'm going to finish school and become a professional perfumer whether you think it's a ridiculous idea or not. I don't care how much money your family has, I don't want to be a housewife. I have a life of my own—goals of my own. I will no longer be controlled or manipulated by you or anyone else. Get it!"

Todd glared at her through angry slits for eyes. "You don't mean any of that!"

"I mean every word."

"Where will you find another man like me? Huh? Someone who is willing to give you everything? You're unappreciative—always have been. The women at home are clamoring for a man like me and you want to throw me away like spoiled meat."

"Hopefully, I won't ever find another man like you. And now that I'm gone, tell Cynthia she can have you!" Shock registered in every muscle across Todd's face. "Yes, I know all about Cynthia. Now she can upgrade her status from cheating sidekick to a real girlfriend for once in her life." Chey felt horrible saying those things, dredging up hurtful memories, but convinced herself that they needed to be said. She still had more to say. Todd closed his gaping mouth. He didn't need to respond; his reaction confirmed everything Chey needed to know. "I won't be like your mother. Sitting around bored out of her mind while your father traipses around the country doing as he pleases with whomever he pleases."

"You…you don't mean that." Todd's mouth twisted in anger. "Take that back!" he stabbed his finger in her direction.

"I won't!"

Todd whirled around and headed for the door. With his hand on the knob, he turned back to scowl at Chey one last time. "When this silly—" he waved his hand around the room "—plan of yours fails, you'll be back. You'd just better hope it's not too late. Maybe I'll have some pity for you and consider still taking you as my wife."

"Don't worry about that, Todd. I could never marry a man I didn't love."

With that, Todd stormed out the door and slammed it hard behind him. Chey could hear him clomping down the steps. She sighed with relief. She didn't have to hide anymore. She was now completely free to live her life as she pleased. No more Todd. No more controlling men, period! Possibly no more well-off men either, since the ones she encountered all seemed to possess the need to control the women in their lives.

She was pressing the restart button, but first she needed to get her mother on the phone to let her know how upset she felt. She couldn't believe Mrs. Rodgers had told Todd where she lived.

Chapter 5

"Ugh!" Hunter wiped his hands down his face in frustration. His grunt rumbled through the villa.

"Let me guess...another delay," Eric, Hunter's frat brother, said as he rolled his suitcase toward the door.

Dave, another of Hunter's frat brothers, scrunched his face, not wanting to add any speculation to the already bad situation. Hunter and Dave, along with Eric and Sam, had just spent the entire week enjoying extreme winter sports on Powder Mountain in Salt Lake City, Utah. Since college, they'd made some kind of adventurous voyage every year, from riding ATVs along the beaches and mountainsides of Costa Rica to Jet Skiing and girl watching off the coast of Rio de Janeiro.

"Yep!" Hunter paced the floor in front of the TV perched over the fireplace, flanked by two mounted moose heads. His hands were positioned at his hips as he tried to think of other ways to get back home to New York City.

Sam, the coolest one of the bunch, sat on the sofa and propped his feet up against the rustic coffee table. "Listen, if you can't get out of here today—" he turned his attention from the TV to Hunter "—just chill for another day or so and head home when the weather calms down a little. You're the boss. Who's going to scold you for not going to work on Monday? Your dad?" His shoulders shook when he laughed.

Sam's casual demeanor was starting to get on Hunter's nerves. "I need to get home ASAP. You wouldn't be saying that if your flight was delayed."

"That's why I moved to sunny Atlanta. We don't have those problems. The weather is hot and the women are, too."

All four men laughed at Sam's last comment. Eric, who lived in Miami, simply shrugged his shoulders as if to say Sam's point was completely valid.

Dave was the only one who offered any kind of sympathy. "Maybe you should just come to the airport and see if you can possibly get another flight. Maybe they could reroute you."

"I don't think it will make a difference. This storm is quickly moving from the Midwest to the East Coast. It's pretty bad. We would be flying right into it. If it weren't for the fact that you were heading to LA before going home to Chicago, you'd be dealing with the same delays."

"Wait! Turn that up?" Sam put his feet down and sat straight up as he pointed to the TV.

Hunter tossed Sam the remote. He didn't want to be the one cranking up the volume on his own misfortune.

"What did he just say?" Sam inclined his ear toward the television.

The four of them abruptly turned their attention to the reporter delivering the breaking news as Sam raised the volume even more. The talking head delivering local news told them that several flights out of Salt Lake City were being canceled.

"Time to go!" Sam jumped to his feet. "I've got some

honeys waiting for me back home. I can't be stuck in this place for another day."

"I haven't seen you move this fast since you thought you saw your ex in that restaurant with another man the last time we were in Atlanta," Eric said, doubled over in laughter.

"Didn't you just tell me not to worry—just take another day?" Hunter mocked, then tossed him a skeptical look.

"I can't get stuck here. Let's get to this airport now!" Sam was at the door with his bags within seconds.

Each body moved with a heightened sense of urgency. Within minutes, all of their bags were at the door. "What are you going to do, man?" Dave asked. "Are you coming with us to the airport?"

"Let me call the airlines. Up until now, I've just been receiving email and text alerts. I need to speak to someone."

Eric looked at his watch. "Get on the horn, man. We can all ride together. I'd hate to leave you here stranded."

"We should all call our airlines to confirm whether or not our flights have been changed or canceled."

They all called their respective airlines, and moments later Eric, Sam and Dave were able to confirm that although there were slight delays, their flights were still scheduled to depart. Hunter, unfortunately, had been told that his flight was canceled and if he was lucky, he might be able to get it rescheduled for some time the next day.

"Aw, man. That sucks," Dave said.

"Hey. It's better to be safe," Eric added.

"You've got another day to chill. Find a way to enjoy yourself," Sam said.

A moment later Eric's phone rang. Their car service had arrived. The men grabbed their bags and headed out of the villa. The cold greeted them with fierce whipping winds as they made their way toward the waiting car. Hunter squinted and turned his head away from the fast-falling snow. A small old man with weathered hands hopped out of the minivan and popped open the back.

With a head nod and a raspy hello, he greeted them one by one as he tried to take their bags to put them in the car. All three of them smiled politely and laid their own bags inside the cargo area.

"What do you think, I'm an old man? I could have done that for you guys," their driver teased.

"We should be driving you around, my man," Eric responded. They all laughed.

When the car was all stocked with their luggage and gear, they turned to Hunter.

"Are you going to be all right by yourself?" Sam asked.

"I'll be fine. I'm going to reception and ask if I can extend my reservation for one more day."

"Don't mean to eavesdrop on your conversation," the driver interjected. The guys looked at one another and smiled. "But did I hear you say you were going to stay one more day?"

"Yes, sir."

He shook his head hard enough for a wisp of gray hair to fall along his brow. "I wouldn't do that if I were you, son. These roads are getting kind of bad. Pretty soon they're gonna close them off. It's dangerous trying to get up and down the mountain when the weather gets really rough."

"But my flight was canceled. I have no choice."

The old man took a deep breath. "Well, just try to make the best of it. They'll probably have room since after a while people won't be able to get up the mountain to get to their lodging. Be safe." Tipping his imaginary hat, he bid Hunter farewell.

Saying their final goodbyes, Hunter tapped the car as they pulled off. Back inside, he called his brothers and parents to update them on the changes in his travel plans. As expected, his mother, Joyce, was worried about him staying overnight in the mountains without a way out.

Hunter headed to the reception area nestled in the center of the villas. He needed to secure accommodations for one more night. When he reached the main cabin, which housed the registration desk, a small café, a full restaurant and a souvenir shop, he realized for the first time that he wasn't the only one on the mountain who had been stranded. The space was filled with frustrated energy. Several people walked circles in the wood floors with cell phones pressed against their ears. Exasperated mothers tried to calm screaming babies, and desk clerks desperately tried to hang on to their dwindling patience as they tried to help riled vacationers.

Hunter spent nearly an hour in line waiting to speak to a clerk, just to find out what he already knew—there was no more room at the inn. However, the clerk agreed to help him as best she could, but he'd have to wait until the arriving guests were placed in rooms. She couldn't guarantee that all of the guests they were expecting would actually make it, but they had to hold their rooms until the evening just in case. Eventually, the road had been shut down, as the old man had predicted, but several guests had indeed made it up the mountain in time. Once the clerks waded through the mayhem, they would have a better idea of whether or not they would have vacancies.

Hunter braved the blistering cold and increasing snowfall as he trudged his way back to the villa to get his bags. He still had his room key. The others had been turned in by his frat brothers. When he got inside, he noticed that housekeeping had already cleaned the room. Instead of rushing back into the cold and waiting around the crowded lobby filled with angry people, he decided to stay in the room. If he was lucky, the person renting his villa might be one of those who hadn't made it up the mountain in time.

After leaving his bags by the door, Hunter flopped on the couch and turned on the TV. The news became graver and after a while all Hunter heard was the droning on of the newscasters as images of maps and heavy snow punctuated their rumblings. Bored, he started flipping through his social media profiles on his phone. When he tired of that, he called and spoke to his brothers again.

For a split second, he thought about calling Tricia and decided against it. He needed to make a clean break when he got back home and didn't want to do anything that could mislead her. He'd managed to avoid most of her calls through the week and when he did pick up, he'd kept his conversations cordial and brief. The last thing he wanted to do was hurt her feelings.

Hunter went back to surfing his profiles until his eyelids grew heavy and he fell asleep.

"Hello!"

A woman's voice broke through his slumber. At first he thought it was part of his dream.

"Excuse me!" The voice was laced with irritation.

Realizing the sound was outside his head, Hunter opened his eyes and beheld the caramel beauty in his blurred vision. With his forefinger, he rubbed his eyes and focused once again. She was still there. He was disoriented for a moment before remembering where he was—in a room that no longer belonged to him.

Hunter jumped up. The woman stepped back.

"I'm sorry. I didn't mean to startle you." He looked around for his bags, blinked and finally got his bearings. "This is your room?"

"Uh…yes!" She held up her set of keys and then folded her arms across her torso.

"Then pardon me…" Hunter paused as his eyes traveled across her sweetheart lips and connected with her large brown eyes. His smile was involuntary. She looked skeptical and slightly confused. "I must have fallen asleep. I didn't mean to alarm you. I'll be out of your way in a moment." He didn't move.

Neither did she.

Their eyes remained connected. Finally, he tore his gaze away from hers and started walking toward his bags by the door. Halfway, he stopped, walked back up to her and held out his hand. "My apologies for being rude. My name is Hunter—Hunter Barrington." At first she hesitated, but then she held out her hand to accept the greeting. Hunter could have sworn the temperature around them rose a few degrees when her hand touched his. He smiled again. "I guess I'll be going now."

Damn, she's gorgeous! Hunter sauntered toward the door, grabbed his bags and walked out into the blanket of snow falling from the Utah evening sky. Only this time, he didn't feel the cold.

Chapter 6

Chey stood frozen in the middle of her floor. Not because of the cold. It was because of the encounter with that stunning stranger who had been sleeping in her villa when she arrived. She felt like Goldilocks even though she was the one who belonged there.

What had he been doing in her room? Who was he? She knew his name—Hunter...Hunter Barrington. She could almost hear him saying it again in that rich baritone timbre.

Despite the fact that his presence had practically scared her senseless, she'd hardly been able to tear her eyes away from his brown skin, dark eyes, inviting lips and tall, lean, muscular frame.

Finally, Chey unglued herself from the spot that she had been standing in since the stranger let himself out.

"Enough with him! I can't believe I'm here!" Chey remembered how excited she was about this solo trip. Giggling, she flopped on the couch. "This feels amazing." She reveled in her freedom. After a deep breath, Chey sank farther into the couch and smiled, but she didn't stay long. After a few moments, she hopped up and went from room to room, checking out her lodging.

The villa resembled a cozy two-bedroom apartment with enough accommodations to sleep up to six people. The rustic Navajo-inspired decor created a warm and cozy vibe that made Chey smile and want to hug herself. On the back wall, there was a vivid view of snowcapped mountains through the large picture window, which looked like an enormous postcard. Chey imagined sitting in front of the stone fireplace, being serenaded by the crackling fire and mesmerized by the glowing embers. She decided right then that that would be her reading spot. The space was more beautiful than she had imagined, even though the hanging moose heads and the life-size bear in the corner proved a little creepy. The common area had an open floor plan, the kitchenette stretching into a great room with an area set aside for a large wood dining table. In front of the leather sofa bed there was a coffee table that looked like a chunk of wood someone had chopped out of a tree and propped on a smaller chunk of wood. Under it, there was a bearskin rug with talons still attached, as if whoever had caught the bear had forgotten to remove the claws. Still, this place was perfect.

Chey hadn't expected the severe weather when she booked this vacation but didn't let that deter her excitement. At some point, she'd get out and do all the adventurous activities she'd planned, but right now all she wanted to do was settle in and relax. Since this was her first time ever doing anything like this, she'd set up lessons for both skiing and snowboarding.

After her self-led tour, Chey called her sister and parents to let them know that she'd arrived safely. Then she went to take a shower. She removed her toiletry bag in search of her facial cleanser, body wash and toothbrush, finding everything except her toothbrush. Frantically, Chey dumped the entire bag on top of the vanity and rummaged through the contents. Then she looked in her purse and finally her suitcase.

Chey groaned, put her fingers to her temple and tried to think. "Where are you, toothbrush?" she asked aloud as if it could answer. Closing her eyes, she concentrated and then realized that she'd left it beside her sink at home. She could see it clearly in her mind. The reception desk would have courtesy toothbrushes, even though she hated those. They didn't feel anything like her electric brush and certainly didn't clean her teeth as well. Maybe when the roads opened, she'd find her way into town and go to a convenience store.

Chey took her time in the shower and then slipped into a pair of comfortable jeans and pulled a knit sweater over her thermal undershirt. Teasing her short tresses, she nudged her curls into place and rubbed her lips with a balm that held a hint of color. Her stomach rumbled and she remembered that the last time she had eaten was before her flight. Grabbing her coat, she put some money into her pocket and headed to the café.

The lobby had cleared out considerably since she'd first arrived. A few people who were obviously still waiting for rooms remained. Some were stretched out in chairs and some lay on the floor with their bags propped up under them.

Chey went to the clerk to ask for the toothbrush and shoved the small courtesy package in her pocket. "Are all these people still waiting for rooms?"

The clerk sighed. "Unfortunately, most of them are stranded and we have no more vacancies. Some of their flights were canceled and others weren't able to get down the mountain before the roads were closed. Some guests have offered to take a few of them in, but there are still several left who don't have a place to stay until at least the morning. We're doing everything we can to find them some kind of lodging. We've set some up in our other resort, but it's pretty much the same situation over there."

"Oh." That was all Chey could say. She felt horrible for them and almost guilty for having so much space to herself. However, as a woman traveling alone, she had to be careful.

Chey thanked the clerk for the toothbrush and headed across the lobby to the café. On her way she spotted the handsome stranger who'd been in her room earlier. Trying to be discreet, she watched him from the corner of her eye as he lay with his head back in a large rocking chair with his feet up on an ottoman. *Damn!* she thought again. He was ridiculously handsome. Just as she crossed in front of him, he lifted his head and attempted to shift his body in the chair. He opened his eyes and Chey quickly turned away. In her peripheral vision, she could see him nestling in his newfound position. He still looked incredibly uncomfortable.

Chey went into the café and ordered a salad and sandwich with a hot cocoa. Her mind kept drifting back to the stranger the entire time she ate and she wondered if he would end up sleeping in that chair all night.

"Excuse me."

It was that voice again. Chey swallowed hard before looking up to acknowledge the person.

"Hi. Can I help you?"

"I was wondering if you would mind if I joined you at your table."

Chey looked around, wondering why he hadn't pursued any other empty seat and quickly realized that there weren't any. The café was full, probably with all the people who had no place to sleep.

Sheepishly, she drew into her shoulders, silently chiding herself for wanting to send him away. The truth was, she couldn't trust herself to be around him without staring as if he were on display at a museum. She assessed him again—smooth brown skin, penetrating eyes, luscious lips framed sharply by a handsome goatee. *Geesh!*

He pleaded with his eyes and then his mouth. "I wouldn't bother you, but there's no place to sit and although I don't know you, I know these other folks even less." He chuckled and the beautiful sultry sound of his laughter made her think of a cool breeze blowing in a meadow at sundown. *How corny!*

Chey pulled her food closer to her side of the table, making room for him to place his food down. He sat directly in front of her and she rolled her eyes before she realized it. She hadn't meant to be rude. She just didn't want the pressure.

Chey allowed herself to look at him and managed a small smile. "Sorry if I seem a little…insolent… I've had such a long day."

"Tell me about it. Whew!" Hunter took a spoonful of his soup and sipped.

Chey watched as his lips puckered to take in the hot liquid. *Mmm!*

"So…" Chey hesitated, not sure if she wanted to actually start a conversation with him. "Are you…stranded?" She braced herself for his answer as if that were a hard question. She felt bad already.

"Unfortunately, yes. I was supposed to go home earlier today, but my flight was delayed and then eventually canceled.

"Oh." What was she supposed to do with that information? She couldn't invite this strange man into her villa. Now she regretted asking him. Chey allowed silence to envelop them. She listened as he quietly sipped his soup.

Part of her wanted to offer him her second room and part of her wanted to stay as far away from him as possible. There was something about him, something that pulled at her, and with her new spontaneous nature, she wasn't sure if that pull would overcome her sense of reason. Secretly she took in his thick silky brows, high cheekbones, bedroom eyes and the strong lines of his chin. This man was chiseled to perfection. She deduced that she probably wasn't his type anyway. She'd noticed his designer luggage. He looked like the type who preferred high-end stilettos, long flowing hair that hit the tailbone, and backgrounds of a certain pedigree. He was probably a wealthy prick like Todd.

Chey found herself wondering if Hunter would find her passion for creating fragrances silly and then cast those thoughts from her mind. Why was she even thinking about such things? "Nice seeing you again…um…?" She pretended to forget his name.

"Hunter," he interjected and held his hand out once again.

Chey shook it and that same feeling from before returned—a slight flutter in her belly.

"Well…" she cleared her throat "…have a good night. I guess I'll see you around."

"I'm sure. Probably right here in the same spot." He chuckled.

"Oh. Sorry," Chey said for lack of anything better. "Good night," she said again.

Chey didn't stop walking until she reached her villa. She pushed the door open, then quickly closed it behind her and leaned her back against it. Why was her heart beating so fast? Why was she flustered? Chey had carefully planned out her day and now that she'd had another encounter with the stranger—Hunter—she was mentally off balance.

Shaking off the feeling that had attached itself to her from the moment he touched her hand again, Chey headed to the first bedroom and pulled out her laptop. She decided to work on her novel. She booted up her computer and started reading through the last chapter she'd written. Every time she read the male character's lines, she imagined Hunter's voice, until finally she put the laptop aside and burst out laughing.

Chey lay back on the comfortable bed and savored the firmness of the mattress as it seemed to mold itself to her body. A vision of Hunter sleeping uneasily in that chair in the lobby popped into her mind. Chey closed her eyes tight in an attempt to rid herself of thoughts of him. She worked at this for some time before rising from the bed, bundling up and heading back to the main reception area to find Hunter, who was now "resting" in a new chair.

"You can have the second room in my villa on one condition."

Chapter 7

It almost didn't matter what condition this brown beauty was about to give Hunter. He was all in. The chair he had been sleeping in had given him a literal pain in his neck and back.

Between uncomfortable naps, he had checked in with the airlines religiously for updates. The flight that he was supposed to go out on in the morning had now been pushed back to sometime in the afternoon. The fact that all of his frat brothers had reached their warmer destinations made Hunter even more miserable. Chey's condition would give him hope if nothing else.

He watched her pretty glossed lips as she spoke.

"I'm working on a very important project and I really need to be able to concentrate. If you can keep distractions to a minimum, then you can have that extra room."

Hunter was ready to follow her to the cozy villa and already anticipated a decent night's sleep. It wouldn't have mattered if she had told him that the condition meant he'd have to sleep hanging from the rafters upside down like a bat; it had to be better than the lobby, which now resembled a New York train station filled with homeless people seeking shelter in the dead of the winter.

Hunter noticed her hesitation even as she offered him the invitation and completely understood.

"I appreciate this very much and will be sure to respect your space. I'll stay out of your way as much as possible. I have to get to the airport early anyway, so hopefully, I won't be too much of a bother." He said what he hoped. If his flight got pushed back any further, he could be looking at another day in the mountains. He'd hate to have to impose on her any further, but after sleeping on the memory foam mattress in the room, he couldn't possibly go back to the hard chair with the worn cushions.

"Agreed?" Chey asked after he was done.

"Huh? Oh. Yes. Agreed!" Hunter took Chey's outstretched hand and shook it vigorously even though he had heard only part of what she'd said. The prospect of sleep took over his mind and senses, but he didn't miss the spark that he felt when he touched her hand again. "I'll keep my noise to a minimum. I'm not a serial killer or a nutcase, so I'll do my best not to creep you out, and I certainly don't mind taking the smaller room." He summed up her statements and tried to reassure her with a little humor at the same time. He also chose to blatantly ignore the electric current that circulated in his gut. He wondered if she'd felt it. Was it real or a figment of his weary mind?

Chey drew in a deep breath and sighed. "Okay. So... let's go."

Chey turned on her boot heel and headed out of the reception area with Hunter and his bags happily in tow.

With Chey walking in front of him, Hunter had a full view of her backside, which curved perfectly. Having no intention of making a move on this considerate woman, despite the fact that she was quite beautiful, Hunter shook his head, shaking away inappropriate thoughts. Tricia came to mind briefly and Hunter was reminded of the fact that he'd just recently written off futile encounters. Not that he was looking to get married, but he no longer wanted to waste time on relationships that he knew wouldn't blossom into something meaningful. Watching his younger brother Blake's and Cadence's relationship bloom made Hunter desire substance over trysts.

Raising a brow, he wondered why the concept of a relationship had even come up with this woman. *Focus. This is just one night.*

"Here we are," Chey said as she opened the villa door. "I was going to have some tea. I can make a cup for you if you'd like."

"I'm fine, thanks. I'll just head to the room and get settled. You will hardly know I'm here," Hunter said. He put his bags in the corner and removed his shoes before returning to the living room. Chey looked down at his sock-covered feet.

"Make yourself comfortable, why don't ya?" She chuckled.

Hunter looked down and laughed. Truthfully, he was quite comfortable since he had just spent the week in that same room. "I guess I already did." The laugh they shared eased some of the tension that engulfed the atmosphere. "Mind if I watch the news? I'll keep the volume low."

Chey shrugged. "Sure. Go ahead. I'll be in my room."

"Thanks!" Hunter grabbed the remote and the TV came to life. It was on the same news channel that he and his frat brothers had watched earlier. The snow wasn't letting up and they were now reporting power outages in the area. The chances of his getting home the next afternoon looked grimmer.

Hunter flopped back on the couch and groaned. With

no laptop, books to read or any real entertainment, he felt caged. Letting the TV stay on for background noise, Hunter flipped through his phone, swiping through social media profiles until he got bored. Getting up from the couch, he walked over to examine the bookshelf, sparsely stocked with complimentary reads. After skimming the few titles that were there and not finding anything of interest, he headed to the kitchen to reheat the leftover water that Chey had used to make her tea.

He went back to the couch and flipped through several channels. Nothing on TV grabbed his attention, so he put the remote down once again. Chey hadn't come out of the room. Hunter wondered what she was doing in there. He flipped back to the news.

Something roared outside the villa. Chey came running into the living room. Hunter stood to his feet.

"Oh my goodness! Was that an animal?" Chey shrieked.

"Actually, I think it was the wind," Hunter replied as he took cautious steps toward the window. The cover of night had made a stormy sky even darker. Hunter couldn't see a thing. When he stepped back from the window, he bumped into Chey, who had been leaning over behind him as he peered through the wood blinds."

"Oopsie." Chey flashed a sheepish grin.

Hunter knew the sound had rattled her. "Maybe I should take a look outside." Chey's evident fear put Hunter in protector mode.

Guardedly, he opened the villa door. The cold wind whirled aggressively as if to push its way inside. Hunter drew back away from the frigid air. He stepped aside, closing the door, and once again bumped into Chey peering over his shoulder. He couldn't help his laugh.

Chey rolled her eyes as if she was embarrassed by her behavior. "Sorry."

"No problem. Let me grab my coat and boots." Hunter stepped around her and retrieved his hat, gloves and coat from the bedroom. "Stay inside," he instructed as he pulled his gloves on before going out into the piercing cold. Taking a quick look around the outside, Hunter didn't see anything threatening. The wind whirled again with a loud rumble, rustling the trees and tossing snow into Hunter's face. Large cold flakes stung his cheeks and filled his eyes so he could hardly see. He felt his way back, and the door opened as soon as he got to it.

Chey stood on the inside. She wiped his face with her hands, helping to clear the snow from his eyes. He felt that spark again. This time he couldn't write it off as part of his imagination. It was definitely real. Again he wondered if Chey felt it, too.

Chey helped him out of his coat, which had been covered in snow in the short amount of time that he'd been outside. Hunter stomped the snow from his feet as Chey shook the wetness from his coat.

"Looks like it's getting worse," she said.

"Yeah!" Hunter blew hot air into his hands and rubbed them together.

"I just hope it passes by in the morning so I can get home."

"Yeah." That was Chey's only response.

For a few moments, they remained close, moving about in an uncomfortable silence.

"Um…here's your coat." Chey held it out toward him.

"Yeah," Hunter said. They danced a few awkward steps around each other as Chey moved one way and then the other trying to get out of Hunter's path to the coatrack.

"I guess I'll get back to work," she finally said.

"Okay." Hunter walked back toward the couch. He really didn't want to go back to being bored, but he also didn't want to bother Chey. "I was going to heat up more water. Would you like more tea?" he asked before she disappeared into the room. It was all he could come up with to make some conversation. The lack of communication was killing him and he was tired of swiping through his timeline on Facebook. He wished he had brought his laptop with him, but he'd insisted on enjoying his vacation and leaving work behind.

"Oh, sure. Let me get my cup." Chey dipped into the room and reappeared quickly.

Hunter walked over to the island where the cooktop was positioned in the center. "It didn't whistle yet, but I'm sure it's hot enough. I'm gonna have hot chocolate. You still want tea?" he said, making a subtle suggestion.

"Hot chocolate sounds good."

Hunter poured two cups and handed the first to Chey.

"Hmm." Chey gripped the mug in both hands, sipped and rolled her head back as she took in the savory sweetness.

"It's good, right?" Hunter said, taking in the lines of her neck.

"Perfect. It's been my favorite since I was a kid," she said with her eyes still closed.

"Yes, it is perfect." Hunter agreed, but he wasn't just referring to the cocoa. Tearing his gaze away from her, Hunter walked over to the couch, sat and started flipping channels again. "Let me know if you'd like another cup. I'll bring it in to you."

"I think I'm done for the night." Chey sat on the arm of the sofa at the opposite end where Hunter was parked. "What are you watching?"

"Just torturing myself with all the weather reports."

"Oh." She slid down onto the couch. "I can imagine.

Bad for you, but I guess it's good for me since I'm scheduled for a ski lesson in the morning."

"You've never skied before?"

Chey sipped her steaming cocoa and shook her head. "First time."

"It's a workout. Look forward to being sore. You'll definitely want to take a nice soak in that supersize tub they have in the bathroom."

"Really! I didn't anticipate that."

"How long are you staying?" Hunter asked, keeping the conversation going. He wanted her to take her time with the cocoa. Not only was her presence fulfilling, but also, he was enjoying the floral scent that wafted from her body and the way her lips puckered and her eyes closed euphorically as she sipped her hot chocolate.

"A week."

"Are your friends joining you tomorrow?"

"No. I'm here…alone."

Hunter noticed her hesitation, assuming that she didn't really want to share that she was vacationing solo—especially with a strange man she'd just met and invited to spend the night in her villa.

"Cool. Brave, but cool." Hunter turned his attention to the TV to keep from staring at her lips. "But why?"

"That's how I planned it. I needed the downtime."

"Hey. Sometimes rolling solo is the only way to do it."

"Yeah." Chey's response hung in the air.

Hunter wanted to know if she was traveling alone because she was single, but he didn't ask.

"Want to watch a movie?" Chey asked, changing the subject and shifting the atmosphere with her cheery tone.

"Sure. I'm not keeping you from getting any work done, am I?"

"No! Pfft." Chey waved away his concern. "I planned

to catch up on a few movies while I was here anyway. I brought a bunch with me—plus, I have Netflix."

Hunter put his mug down and stood. "Cool. There's a DVD player here and cables to connect devices. What would you like to watch?"

"Be right back." Chey put her mug down and ran to the room to retrieve her movies and iPad. "Okay," she said as she was heading back. "I have *The Best Man Holiday*, which you probably don't want to watch, and I have *Avengers: Age of Ultron*."

"Seriously!" Hunter chuckled. "You like the Avengers?"

"Absolutely." Chey looked at Hunter as if he'd asked a ridiculous question.

"Whichever you want to watch, I'm fine with. It's your call, since you're supplying the entertainment."

Chey sat on the opposite end of the couch and folded her legs. "Let's start with *Best Man* and if you can hang, then we will watch *Avengers*. Deal?"

"That sounds like a challenge and I like challenges." Hunter wondered if Chey picked up on his innuendo.

Chey laughed, and for some reason, it was the sweetest sound Hunter remembered hearing in his thirty-two years. He reached for the DVDs that Chey held in her hand and did the honors of setting up the first movie. Chey went to her room and grabbed two bags of popcorn and placed them in the microwave.

For the next few hours, they laughed at the antics of the characters from both movies. When Chey got teary eyed from the sad scenes in *The Best Man Holiday*, Hunter fought the urge to pull her into his arms and wipe away her tears. By the time the movies were done, Hunter fought sleep just to continue spending time in Chey's presence. As she grew more comfortable around him, conversation flowed more easily and she sat closer to him on the couch. There was something about this woman that Hunter liked.

When they finally retreated to their respective rooms, Hunter checked his phone and found that he had missed a few calls from Tricia. He was glad he had left his phone in the bedroom. Then he wondered if Chey had anyone calling her and assumed that she probably didn't, since she was here vacationing alone. In the morning, he'd try to find out more about the mysterious Chey.

Chapter 8

Chey woke with a start, looked around the room and re-membered that she wasn't at home. Memories of watch-ing movies with Hunter brought a smile to her face. She pulled back the covers, got out of the bed and headed to the adjoining bathroom. As she showered, she wondered if Hunter was awake.

After dressing again in layers with jeans and a thick sweater, Chey walked quietly to the kitchen for a cup of coffee. To her surprise—and delight—Hunter had already prepared a pot of coffee and laid out several selections for breakfast on the table.

"Good morning!" he said and smiled. She could have sworn she saw his perfect teeth sparkle.

"Good morning to you. I see you're up and ready to go."

"I'm going home today!"

A twinge of sadness sprang up in Chey. She was start-ing to enjoy his company. "Oh! Did it stop snowing?" she asked, then walked toward the window and peered out at the snow still falling."

"Nope!" Hunter said with confidence.

Chey raised a brow. "Uh…"

Hunter walked toward her with one of the steaming cups. "I'm being hopeful. Coffee?"

"Sure!" Chey took the cup with her brow still raised and followed Hunter with her eyes as he made his way over to the large dining table.

"As a token of my appreciation, I took the liberty of getting breakfast. You could have left me in the lobby last night. I couldn't imagine having to sleep in that chair all night long. I wasn't sure what you'd want, so I brought a few options." He held up packages of cream and sugar. "I didn't know how you liked your coffee, so these are for you, and in case you didn't like coffee, I also have picked up tea."

Chey nodded her approval. "How considerate!" She looked over the options. "I'll take the egg sandwich. Thanks!"

Hunter pulled out a chair and gestured for Chey to have a seat before sitting on the opposite side.

"Such a gentleman," she said, shaking a package of raw sugar.

"I try." Hunter flashed that smile again and something squiggled in her chest.

Was that my heart skipping a beat? What the heck! Chey kept a smile on her face for Hunter's sake and then set an intent focus on opening her egg sandwich. What was happening?

They ate in silence for several moments.

"What—?" Both of them started at the same time.

"Sorry. You go first," Chey said.

"No!" Hunter shook his head adamantly. "Ladies first."

"I was going to ask, what time is your flight?"

"It was supposed to leave around one, but now I'm seeing that it's been pushed back to five in the evening."

Chey sucked in air. "Oh."

"Yeah. I know. What time is your ski lesson?"

"Nine." Chey looked at her watch. "I have about forty-five minutes. I hope they don't cancel it because of the weather."

"You should be fine."

Silence swelled between them for another few moments. Chey thought about asking Hunter if he wanted to join her on the slopes since he had so much time before leaving. Then she decided not to waste her time. What sense did it make getting to know him when she would probably never see him again? Then again, it would be nice to have some company.

"What time are you heading to the airport?"

"Don't worry. I'll be out of your hair very soon. I just wanted to make sure you enjoyed your breakfast."

Chey held her hand up. "I didn't mean it that way. I was just wondering how you planned to pass the time. It's still pretty early and you don't have to be at the airport until later this afternoon. That's even if you are still able to get out of here today."

Hunter sighed. "As long as the roads are open, I can find something to do."

"Want to join me on the slopes?" There. She'd asked.

"That's not a bad idea, but I don't do bunny slopes, though."

Chey playfully rolled her eyes. "Hey! It's my first time."

"I'm sure you're a quick learner."

Chey chuckled. "We'll see. So what do you say? Slopes or nah?"

"Slopes it is!"

Another twinge shot through Chey. This time it was excitement.

"Before I go, I just need to check in with the airlines and find some transportation to the airport."

"Cool." Chey took the last bite of her sandwich, clapped the crumbs from her hand and cleaned the area with a napkin. "I'll be ready in ten minutes," she said, pushing back from the table.

"I'm going to jump on the phone."

Chey left Hunter to handle his business as she got everything together for her first skiing lesson. Exhilaration whirled through her, giving her more vigor than the coffee. Hunter was going to be around for another few hours and she liked the idea of spending more time with him. She was glad to have his company.

As Chey pulled out the gloves that she'd bought especially for this trip, she heard Hunter groan. The sound bellowed through the villa and seemed more like an animal's growl. Chey grabbed her things and jogged to the great room, where Hunter stood with the phone to his ear and his other hand firmly planted on his forehead.

With her expression she asked, *What happened?*

Hunter frowned, briefly closed his eyes and shook his head.

Chey left him to his call and continued getting her stuff together. By the time she came back to the great room, Hunter was pacing.

"Bad news, I assume."

"The flight was pushed back another hour, but that's not the worst of my problems." Chey frowned as she awaited the additional news. "The roads are still considered unsafe and even if I could catch my flight, I'm unable to get to the airport!" Hunter huffed and let his head fall back.

"I'm so sorry. How long do they anticipate the roads being closed?"

"They don't know. The snow has been falling for almost twenty-four hours straight. They can't start trying to clear them until the snow stops or at least slows down some. They said it's one of the worst storms the area has seen in years."

"Oh, no! I wonder if my ski lesson will be canceled."

"Maybe you should call. In the meantime, I'll check in with reception to see if there's any chance that I can get into another room, even if I have to share with another guest. Either way, I'll be out of your hair today."

Chey didn't want him out of her hair.

"Listen, don't worry. You can have the room another night if you need. I don't mind."

"Are you sure? I don't want to impose."

Chey waved off his look of concern. "I've already spent one night with a complete stranger—what's another night?"

At least she made Hunter smile, and again that twinge danced in her belly.

"I'll pay for these two nights. Thanks."

"No need. I didn't think I'd enjoy your company, but I do." Chey froze, sorry that she'd been so brutally honest—a "problem" she'd developed when she freed herself of Todd.

"Okay?" Hunter responded as if he wasn't sure how to take her comment.

She was slightly ashamed at her bluntness. "I'm sor—"

Hunter put his hands up, stopping her. "No need to apologize. That's how you really feel. I have always appreciated people who weren't scared to be forward."

"Shall we see if the slopes are open?" Chey was happy to change the subject. Calling the front desk, she tried to find out about her lesson. After being passed around a few times, she finally confirmed that the lesson and all other activities had been canceled for the day due to the weather. Besides the fact that the weather conditions made the activities unsafe, many of the instructors lived in the area and were unable to get to work.

Chey was disappointed but tried to stay positive. "I guess I'll work on my book and catch up on some reading and more movies."

"Let me know if you feel like company. I saw that they have a few board games on the bookshelf over there."

"Hmm. That could be a fun way to pass some time." Chey started toward the bookshelf. "What do they have?" Sitting on the floor, she looked through the games. "Oh! Scrabble! That's my favorite. Monopoly. Yahtzee. Taboo. Oh, and 5 Second Rule!" She hoisted herself up on one hand. "Oh my goodness. I love this game. It's so much fun. Let's play this." Chey carried the game to the table.

"I've never heard of that game."

"Really? My family and I play this all the time. It's easy. I'll show you." Chey spread the board out on the table and shuffled the cards. "Basically, you have five seconds to name three things in a specific category. We'll do a test run." Chey gave a few examples, all of which Hunter fumbled, failing to get his answers out during the five seconds allotted. Each time the buzzer went off, signifying another unsuccessful attempt, he groaned. By the third try, both he and Chey were doubled over in laughter.

"This is embarrassing. I'm a lawyer. I'm supposed to be able to think fast on my feet! Set that timer!" Hunter pointed to the small object. "Let's see how well you do."

"Come with it! I've got this!" Chey welcomed the challenge.

Hunter asked the first question and pressed his face closer to Chey's, waiting for her answer. She tried to think fast. Answer fast. Hunter's face was inches from hers. She laughed. Then stuttered, snapped her fingers and then fumbled. The timer buzzed.

"Ha! See! And you were laughing at me."

"That's not fair. You made me laugh."

"That was strategy!"

Chey gasped and tossed one of the couch pillows decorated with scenes of mountain wildlife. "That's cheating!"

"No. That's winning!" Hunter sang in true Charlie Sheen fashion.

"Okay, Hunter. It's on!" Chey took on a competitive stance and pulled out a new set of cards. "You ready? Let's go!"

Hunter leaned in, matching her stance. "Ready."

Hunter fumbled his way through an entire round, hardly able to speak because he was laughing so hard. Chey managed to get a few answers in before the buzzer went off and declared herself the undisputed winner. Chey victory-danced around the table with her fists in the air. She bobbed and weaved and rubbed her win in Hunter's face.

Hunter sat back and smiled, entertained by her clowning around.

"Oh, I'm sorry." Chey feigned innocence. "I don't mean to be a sore winner. Boo-yah!"

They cackled for what seemed like forever. Each time their laughter subsided, they'd start up all over again. It took several minutes for them to reel themselves in.

Finally, Hunter went back over to the bookshelf and came back with a deck of cards.

"I Declare War?" he challenged her, holding up the deck.

"What do you know about that game?" She twisted her lips and shot him an amused look.

"My brothers and I played that all of the time."

"No. I want to play a game of Spit! What do you know about that?"

"Oh! I'm the master at Spit! I was the only one able to beat my dad. Are you sure you want to play with me? I never lose."

"Is that a challenge?" Chey put her hand on her hip. "Because you've never played with me."

"Be careful," Hunter said with all confidence.

Chey sucked her teeth, dismissing his warning. "I Declare War, then Spit. Now deal the cards!" she commanded.

With a slick smile, Hunter split the deck in half and then counted to make sure they each had an equal number of cards. For the next hour, Chey was lost in the sheer joy of playing nostalgic games that had been some of her family's favorite pastimes—games that her father had taught her and her sister as children. Games that Todd would have never spent time playing with her, because he would have been too busy declaring them silly wastes of time. She won two rounds of I Declare War and boasted hard.

They switched to Spit, and Hunter was too fast for her. After losing the first game, she insisted that he'd cheated and challenged him to another game. She lost that one, too. Her hand tingled from his touch when they reached for the same pile of cards and his hand landed on top of hers. They lingered there, the masculine feel of his palm covering the back of her hand sending currents up her arm and straight to her belly, releasing a gang of butterflies. Their eyes met and connected. A beat passed. Then two. She cleared her throat. Slowly he lifted his hand and she pulled hers out from under his.

"Movie?" she asked when she was able to find her words.

"Sure." Hunter held her in his view with the same level of intensity as he had when his skin touched hers.

Chey cleared her throat again. "I'll go get them." When she got to her room, she closed the door, shut her eyes and breathed.

Chapter 9

By the time the sun made its full ascension the next morning, Hunter had already called the airlines, checked on the mountain roads and called the concierge to see if he and Chey would be able to indulge in any of the winter sporting activities. The snow had finally taken a break, but the number of trees that had fallen left the main roads even more unsafe. The airlines were taking reservations, but with the thousands who had been stranded, many of whom had beaten him to the phone, he couldn't get confirmed on a flight until the next afternoon. This meant he'd have to spend a third night at the resort and pray without ceasing in hopes that roads would finally be safe enough for him to travel home tomorrow.

Blake interrupted his flow when he called for an update.

"You're up early." Hunter flicked the television off.

"Coming home today, bro?"

"No!" Hunter sighed, but wasn't as perturbed as he pretended to be. He looked forward to spending another day with Chey. It had taken all of his willpower to resist stroking her supple skin and shiny black hair when she fell asleep across his lap after the third movie.

"Seriously? You must be going crazy. I'd lose it…" Blake whistled, punctuating his point. "Where's the honey that let you stay in her villa?"

Hunter looked toward her room before whispering, "I think she's still sleeping. She hasn't come out of her room."

"You think she'll have a problem with you staying another night?"

"Hope not." Hunter looked up again to ensure that she hadn't made an appearance.

"So are you going to get her number?"

"Probably not. I don't do the long-distance thing."

"Where does she live?"

Hunter thought for a moment. "Actually, I don't know. Never asked." Hunter pondered the fact that with all the time they'd spent together in the past two days, there was still much he didn't know about her.

"Keep me posted and let me know if you need a ride from the airport tomorrow."

"What's up at the office?"

"Worry about that when you get back. I've got everything covered. I need to get to work. Talk to you later."

Hunter ended the call, retreated to his room and changed into something comfortable enough to exercise in. He needed to work through the pent-up tension in his muscles. Partly from his horrible travel ordeal and partly from the fact that he wanted to touch Chey in sacred places so bad that his muscles ached—very specific muscles.

Trying to stay quiet, Hunter took to the floor in front of the fireplace and cranked out a couple of push-ups, sit-ups, planks and mountain climbers. Then he took to the sturdy coffee table for a few triceps dips. As he reached his last set, Chey came out of her room looking ripe with natural beauty.

Her eyes stretched at the bulging in his arms and Hunter added another set of ten dips for good measure.

"Morning, Hunter."

He could see through his peripheral vision that Chey had been staring at him. "Oh." Grunt. "Hey." He acted as if he'd just noticed her. Jumping up, Hunter wiped the sweat from his hands down the front of his basketball shorts and stretched his arms.

"Looks like you've been up for a while." Chey made her way to the kitchen. "Have you eaten?"

Feeling pumped, Hunter took off his shirt and wiped the sweat from his head and neck.

The move wasn't necessary, but it did serve his purpose. He hadn't missed the way Chey's brows slightly lifted.

"Nah. I usually don't eat before working out."

"Oh." Chey put the coffeepot on and yawned.

"I'll run and get something for us from the café."

"I'll walk over with you. I could use the change of scenery." Silence descended on the room once again.

Chey was distant this morning. The day before, silence hadn't stood a chance. Hunter watched as she moved around the kitchen cautiously. He decided to give her some space. He went into his room to shower.

When he got back, Chey was sitting on the couch tuned into the morning news.

"The roads are still closed! Can you believe this?" She spoke to him but kept her eye on the news reporter. "Have you spoken to the airline?" She turned to him with concern etched in the lines of her face.

Hunter threw his hand up. "Flights are starting to go out, but they couldn't confirm me on anything before tomorrow afternoon." Flopping on the couch, he continued, "If I could get to the airport, I could try to get on the list for standby, but they said that wasn't guaranteed and with the amount of people that are trying to get out, it would probably be a waste of time."

"I just heard on the news that there are trees down all along the roads. Crews are working on cleaning them up now, but that will take hours, maybe even days. You must be so annoyed."

"Yeah." *Not really.*

"You can certainly stay another night if need be."

"I appreciate that."

Chey got up and headed for the landline. "I wonder if I can get my lesson today. You can join me," she said over her shoulder.

"I already called." Chey stopped walking. Her shoulders slumped. "Yeah," Hunter continued, confident that she already knew what he was about to say. "That's a no-go once again."

"Ugh!" She practically stomped back to the couch, her inner child clearly getting the best of her. "I'll never learn to ski." She picked up the remote and cranked up the volume. I guess you're stuck with me for another day, although I should try to get some work done on that book."

"I can take care of myself. Do what you have to do."

The coffeemaker gurgled and sent a rich aroma through the villa. Chey got up and poured two cups without hesitating, handing one to Hunter as if it were a familiar dance that she'd done for years.

Hunter took the cup and sipped, grimaced from the heat and said, "Thanks."

"Let's get breakfast and after that, I can come back and work on my book. You can go through my movies or check out Netflix and see if there's anything you want to watch. I feel so bad that you've been stranded for so long."

Chey and Hunter bundled up in order to brave the cold for the short walk to the restaurant in the main reception area. What they saw when they walked outside stopped them both. In unison, they gasped, their mouths hanging agape. This storm was much worse than they'd realized. Several of the resort's towering trees were now stretched across the grounds just yards from their door. Some leaned as if they were still deciding whether or not to fall. One tree had even broken through the roof of one of the nearby villas. Debris tumbled across the walkway, being shoved by the still-strong winds. Snow from rooftops flew horizontally, causing them to shield their faces.

Inside the lobby, people were pacing, talking on cell phones, raising their voices at the front-desk clerks, whose irritation now hid behind thin veils of patience. Kids cried. Parents sighed and bounced babies in their arms. Hunter and Chey silently maneuvered through the crowd, in awe of the scene unfolding around them. Hunter looked down and didn't remember when he had taken Chey's hand in his. At the restaurant, their thirty-minute wait expanded into a fifty-minute one. Thankful they weren't dealing with as much obvious frustration as some of their fellow guests, they exercised the utmost patience with every resort employee they encountered.

Breakfast was consumed mostly in silence, save a few brief inquiries by their waitress and some forced small talk between the two of them. That same silence dominated their walk back to the villa.

Once inside, Chey shook her head. "Wow! I had no idea."

"Neither did I." Hunter took a seat on the stool near the counter that divided the kitchen from the main space.

Chey walked toward the picture window centered in the back wall. Folding her arms across her chest, she shook her head. "Wow! Looks can truly be deceiving. I mean look at this view. It's so beautiful," she sighed. "Peaceful. I never would have guessed all this mayhem lay in wait right outside the front door!"

Chey walked back over and sat on a stool next to Hunter. "I have been looking forward to this vacation for months. I couldn't wait to go skiing and snowboarding and take the shuttle into town to eat and do some souvenir shopping for my family and then write by the fire. I really hope this gets better before it's all over."

"I'm sorry things aren't going the way you expected."

Chey clucked her tongue. "No. I'm sorry. Here I am complaining and you've been trying to get home for the past two days. There's still hope for me." Chey sucked in a lungful of air and blew it out. She turned to face Hunter. "How was your trip before—" she waved her hand around "—all of this?"

"My frat brothers and I did all those things that you're looking forward to doing. We hung out in town, rented snowmobiles, skied. We're pretty adventurous."

"That sounds like fun. I guess I'll have to live my vacation vicariously through you. Tell me more."

Hunter obliged her curiosity, sharing stories about their adventures, as well as ones he'd engaged in with his brothers. He was happy to put a smile on her face. Since she had opened up a little, he decided to ask her a few questions.

"So why are you here alone?"

"Whoa! That was subtle," Chey teased and raised her brows.

"A beautiful woman like you?" Hunter relished in the reddish hue that warmed her cheeks, brought on by his compliment. "Why travel alone?"

"This is part celebration, part test."

"What are you testing?"

"My ability to live life on my own…and on my own terms."

"Bad breakup?"

"Kind of." Chey turned away.

"Wanna talk about it?"

"Not really." Chey paused. "Let's just say our expectations weren't lining up."

Hunter took a slight turn in his line of questioning in order to keep her talking.

"So where are you from?"

"A small town several miles outside Woodbridge, Virginia."

"I have a cousin in Woodbridge. I grew up in a big city. I always wondered if I could do small-town living."

"And I often wondered what it would be like to live in a big city. It always seemed so intriguing."

"Any brothers or sisters?"

"One sister." Chey didn't look at him as she answered. He could tell she didn't want to reveal too much, but he was eager to know more about her.

"What do you do?"

"Right now I'm a student—again."

"Again?"

"Yeah. I took some time off to help my parents out. They have a great little shop in our area. We try to bring our small-towners a few big-city options. Now that the store is doing better, I've decided to go back and finish school."

"What do you sell?"

"Mainly clothes and accessories, but it's kind of like a variety store. My mom crochets and we get a decent amount of orders during the holidays or when someone has a baby. We also sell some of my dad's favorite cigars, as well as scented candles, fragrances and a few home-decor items.

"Cool! What are you studying in school?"

"Chemistry."

Hunter stretched his eyes. "Wow. So you're pretty smart," he chuckled.

"Silly!" Chey laughed. "I guess I am." She wiggled proudly.

"Hey, how about we watch another movie? I have more popcorn." Chey stretched her eyes as if she were giving him the offer of the century.

Hunter took the hint. She was done talking. "Sounds good. As long as you don't fall asleep on me again." Hunter's core almost responded to the memory of her sleeping in his lap.

"I guess I wasn't very good company last night." Chey stood from the stool. "Speaking of which, I don't even remember going to my room and getting in bed," she laughed. "When I got up this morning, I wondered how I got there. You would have thought I was drinking." She seemed tickled by her words.

"I carried you."

"Huh?" Chey inclined her ear toward Hunter, still chuckling. "What did you say?"

"I said…" Hunter's purposeful pause was designed to make sure that she heard him "…I carried you."

Chapter 10

Saved by the ring! "Excuse me." Relief shrouded Chey as she reached for her cell phone and shot off to her room to speak in private. Her insides had warmed when he said that he'd carried her to the room.

"Girl! Your timing couldn't have been better," she told her sister, Deanna, the second she answered.

"What happened?"

"Remember the sexy…" Chey peeked toward the door to make sure Hunter was out of earshot "…stranger I told you about?"

"Yes, crazy. The one you let stay in the villa with you. I still have the picture of him in my phone from when you texted me the other day. If your behind came up missing, I was going to send that sucker to ABC News! Shoot! I must admit, he was handsome as hell. Does he know you took that picture?"

"Heck, no! The flash was off and I acted as if I was checking my hair. I actually took several pictures. The one I sent to you was one of the best." Chey thought for a moment. "You didn't tell Mom and Dad, did you?" Chey felt her heart race a bit at the thought. Prone to worry, her mother would have a fit if she knew Chey allowed a stranger to sleep in her villa and she was traveling alone. "I didn't mention it when I spoke to her and I don't want you to either."

"I didn't say a word. Get back to what happened."

Chey told her about how much she enjoyed their time together the day before and how he'd just told her that he'd carried her to bed last night. She also filled her in on all the mayhem the storm had caused and the fact that she still hadn't done any skiing.

"Wow. Every time I speak with you, there's a new adventure. I don't need reality TV anymore. When I need a little dose of crazy or some 'you won't believe this' to heighten my day, I'm going to call you from now on."

"Hush it, silly. Anyway. He's staying another night."

"Hmm. Are you sure about that?"

"He's been here for the last two nights. What's going to happen tonight?"

"I don't know. I guess I'll have to wait for the report tomorrow."

"Anyway!" Chey chided her sister. "I'm hoping to finally get on the slopes tomorrow." Chey changed the subject and they chatted about her upcoming visit home during spring break. When they were finished, Chey called and spoke with her parents while gathering the other movies she'd promised to get from her carry-on bag. She'd kept Hunter's presence a secret from them. Chey couldn't possibly tell them she was sharing her villa with a strange man.

Purposely, Chey left all of the romantic comedies behind and brought only the action flicks out for their enjoyment. She didn't want Hunter getting any ideas, even though she'd already imagined what it would be like to kick caution to the curb and become intimate with him. If he made a move, would she resist? Hmm. From the way he looked at her, she knew he wanted her as much as she would have liked to try him out. The sexual tension crackled louder than the logs in the fireplace. She had already imagined what it would be like to feel his lush lips on hers. She was borderline upset about the fact that he'd carried her in his strong arms and she didn't even remember. She'd never be able to reminisce about what it felt like to be in his arms. What a waste!

Chey shook those thoughts from her head and went back into the living room. She stepped slowly and quietly when she realized that he was on the phone. Laying the movies out on the coffee table, she waited patiently for him to finish. Based on the professional tone of his voice, she assumed the call was about business.

"Hey!" Hunter placed his hand on her shoulder.

Chey jumped. She had been so engrossed in going through the movie selections that she hadn't heard him approach. His touch startled and excited her.

"I didn't mean to scare you. I was just letting you know I was off the phone." Hunter rounded the couch and sat. Leaning forward, he scanned the movies. "Now, what are our choices?"

"You pick this time." Chey spread the movies farther apart so that titles would show clearly.

"Whoa! You have the first *Iron Man*?" Hunter beamed. "That's one of my favorite movies."

"Me too! Let's watch it. You do the honors—" Chey handed him the DVD "—while I pop the popcorn."

Together they stood and proceeded to fulfill their designated duties.

"I actually have all of the *Iron Man* movies. I thought I brought them with me, but it seems I only have that one." Chey unfolded the bag of popcorn and placed it in the microwave and then leaned on the counter waiting for it to pop.

"I haven't met many women who enjoy these kinds of movies."

"You've never met me." She was testing this flirting thing out and decided she enjoyed it.

Hunter stopped what he was doing and cast a smoldering gaze with one brow raised. "I know you now." The timbre of his voice had fallen a few octaves. The bellow tickled her core.

"Well, there's a lot you still don't know," she teased.

"And we can fix that."

Either the room got warmer or someone had set a match inside her belly. The microwave dinged, saving her from trying to think of a comeback. Hunter winked and turned his attention back to the DVD.

Chey poured the popcorn in a bowl and joined Hunter on the couch. Halfway into the movie they heard a loud crack, a pop and then a substantial boom. The TV fizzled and went black. The time on the DVD player flashed and then disappeared. Both of them sat straight up.

"Oh my goodness! What was that?" Chey didn't realize the grip she had on Hunter's arm until he tried to pry himself free to go and explore the issue.

Chey let go, hoping she hadn't broken any skin with her nails. Picking up the remote, she randomly pushed buttons in an attempt to get the TV to come back on. Then she stood, went to the TV and hit the power button several times. Nothing happened. Once again Hunter threw on his coat and went outside to assess the situation. Chey could hear him talking to someone but couldn't make out what he was saying.

She ran to her room, got her coat and met Hunter outside. He was talking with a neighbor from a nearby villa who was apparently just as clueless as he was. People were coming out of their rooms with puzzled looks that matched hers and Hunter's.

"I'm going to reception to find out what's happening. Go back inside and I'll be right back." Protectively, he covered her hand with his before trotting off.

Inwardly, she smiled. She liked Hunter's protective nature.

Chey stayed outside chatting with another guest for a few moments before heading back inside. Walking around the villa, she checked to see if there was power in any of the rooms. She found none. Chey collapsed on the couch, moaned and fell over, pressing the side of her face in the cushions.

"What else could go wrong?" Immediately, she sat up. "I didn't mean that!" She looked toward the ceiling, knowing that was the worst question one could ask in a crisis.

Unable to remain still, Chey went back to the door and looked out. More people had come out, but there was no sign of Hunter yet. She went back inside and absentmindedly filled the teakettle with water and tried to turn on the electric stove. Nothing happened. "Ugh!"

Chey sat on the stool and pulled out her cell phone. She called Deanna, who answered after a few short rings.

"You won't believe this!"

"What happened now?" Deanna's tone was anxious.

"We were watching a movie and heard these loud noises and then the power went out. Hunter went out to find out what happened."

"What else could go—?"

"Uh, uh, uh! Don't you say it! You ask that and I'll probably find out."

"You're right! I'll swallow those words. I'm starting to get worried."

"It's just the storm. I'll be fine. Hopefully, they'll have the electricity up and running soon."

"Well, keep me posted."

"I will."

When Chey hung up her phone, she looked at her battery and noted she had 70 percent. She hoped that the power would return before her battery died. In the meantime, she'd have to use her phone sparingly. Chey tapped her home key twice and closed all the apps running in the background. Then she returned to the couch to wait for Hunter.

Several moments later, Hunter came bustling through the door, bringing in a rush of cold air and several logs of wood with him. Chey stood.

"The power's out." Hunter dropped the wood to his feet and peeled himself out of his coat.

"I already figured that out, silly. Why is it out?"

After tossing his coat on the rack, Hunter grabbed the logs and placed them by the fireplace. He slapped his hands against his jeans to rid them of the sawdust.

"Remember we saw a few trees that looked like they were leaning?" He didn't give her time to answer. "Well, one of them decided to fall, pulling down power lines and smashing into one of the main generators. This whole side is without power and they aren't sure exactly when it will be back up."

"Ugh!" Chey had groaned more in the past two days than she had in the past two years. "I can't believe this. What else—?"

Hunter held up his hand, silently beseeching her not to finish that sentence.

Chey rolled her eyes and dropped her head. "You're right," she said, acknowledging his attempt to keep her from finishing that taboo sentence once again.

Hunter looked at his phone. "I'm down to 50 percent. What are you on?"

"Seventy percent. Make sure you close out all your apps and turn off your cellular data and roaming."

"I've already done that."

With the heat out, a chill was already settling over the villa.

"Let me get this fire started and then I'll run back to reception to get more firewood. They're handing it out to guests now."

When Hunter had left to get more wood, Chey fashioned a cozy setting in front of the fireplace with blankets and pillows. A romantic atmosphere was not her intent, but that was what it ended up looking like. She sat in the center of the space she'd created and let the warmth of the fire caress her skin while the crackle of the wood charmed her ears.

Hunter returned and joined her on the floor. Without cell phones, DVDs, laptops or any other power-operated devices to engage them, they were left to entertain each other. They talked until a companionable silence took over.

"What was he like? Was he a nice guy?" Hunter said, obviously referring to Chey's ex.

She laughed. "You're nosy." She held out another moment. "No. He wasn't that nice."

"Is that why you broke up?"

"Actually, no. I wanted more out of life than he was willing to contend with."

"He was a dream killer," Hunter summed up matter-of-factly.

"A dream killer?" Chey craned her head toward him.

"Yeah. The kind of person that tries to kill your ideas while you're sharing them. You know, they ask questions like 'Why would you want to do that?'"

Hunter had Todd pegged. Suddenly, Chey felt more connected to him and wondered what Hunter would have to say about her dream of becoming a perfumer. Would he think it was silly?

"Then that's exactly what he was," Chey finally agreed.

"Too bad."

"What about you, Mr. Nosy? You have a woman back home?" Her curiosity got the best of her. She had told herself not to bother getting to know him.

"No. There's no woman back home."

"Why?"

"I guess the right one has yet to come along."

"Oh."

"What do you do?"

"Mostly litigation. But I dabble in other areas of law, as well."

"I guess you're pretty smart, too."

Both of them chuckled and continued chatting until the sun departed, leaving them to the light of the moon through the picture window and the embers glowing in the fireplace.

The coolness of the villa had forced them to draw closer to the fire and each other. Chey's back settled against Hunter's chest as they both watched the embers dance in the shadows.

"Is this how you imagined your liberating solo vacation would turn out?"

"Not at all."

"Me neither." Hunter sniffed out a chuckle. "This is actually better than I thought it would be."

Chey craned her neck, tossing Hunter a baffled look.

"I never thought I'd end up with a beautiful woman in my arms as we sat in front of a fireplace with a view of mountains beckoning at my side."

Chey's cheeks burned. She turned back toward the fire

and let her head settle in the center of Hunter's chest. No words were necessary. Hunter was right. Despite all that had gone wrong, she could have never called this and was grateful that she didn't have to endure this alone. What would she have done if Hunter had made his flight home on the first day?

"You smell amazing." Hunter's voice had reduced to a husky whisper.

"Thank you." Chey smiled but didn't turn around. "It's one of my creations." If Hunter kept it up, they would no longer need the fireplace for heat.

"You made that?"

"Yep."

"That's some talent." She felt Hunter nod.

"You don't smell so bad yourself," Chey teased.

"Thanks!" Silence. Then laughter.

As the laughter subsided, Chey noticed how Hunter instinctively rubbed her arm. His touch alone was enough to keep her warm.

Eventually the quiet of the night expanded and settled over them like a soft blanket. They nestled into the inviting softness, connecting without words. Chey enjoyed the moment in the midst of all the chaos but longed for more. She wanted Hunter to touch her in other places. She wanted to feel him. The longer she sat there in his arms, the more desire stirred inside her.

Chey's conscious fought over her desire and the reality of her knowing Hunter for only a short while. Never before had she been in such a compromising battle with her will. She had spent most of her dating years with Todd and had had only a few suitors before that. She'd never felt as if she'd belonged in any of their arms, yet being cradled by Hunter seemed so right. One-night stands weren't even in her vocabulary, but something in her trampled all reason and urged her to throw caution to the treacherous winds and indulge herself completely in this gorgeous man.

Heck! What did she have to lose? All she needed to do was protect herself and she was sure he'd come prepared with the necessary paraphernalia. Once he got on that flight, she'd never see him again anyway. No awkward run-ins. No phone calls necessary. This was her time to explore life in a way that she'd never done before. She decided right then, if he'd have her, she'd give her all to him tonight.

Chey twisted her head, looking up at Hunter, watching the flames of the fire twinkle in his brown eyes. He looked down at her. They stayed that way for a while, locked in each other's gazes, until Hunter broke the stare, leaned in and kissed her on her lips. When his lips touched hers, she felt light, as if she were floating. The dam holding back the remnants of her cautious nature broke. Chey turned her body, wrapping her arms around his neck, and Hunter explored the deepest crevices of her with his tongue, moaning. They kissed until they ran out of breath, broke free and kissed again and yet again.

Hands roamed sacred places. Blinding desire raised hairs on arms, creating sensually rocky terrain. Clothing was carefully discarded until there was skin against skin. Hunter pulled her into him until she couldn't be pulled in any further. Warm bodies meshed, trying desperately to become one.

Hunter pulled back, searching Chey's eyes for permission to proceed. Eager pleading flashed in his brown orbs. "Do you want this?" His voice dipped low and sultry from fierce longing.

Granting him approval with a nod and another deep, sensual kiss, Chey grabbed his face and drew him to her hungry lips. Any closer and she would have passed through him if it were possible. Hunter gently laid her back on the blanket beneath them and positioned himself next to her, propped on one elbow. First he lavished her with a slow once-over, smiling. Then he touched the places he'd studied with wonder, as if he didn't believe they were real— eyes, lips, neck, shoulders, breasts, nipples. They pebbled. He continued his passionate probe. Stomach, navel, the outskirts sheltering her pearl, inner thighs, knees, toes. Replacing his finger with his tongue, he retraced that same path. Chey's skin seared from this touch.

He kissed her again, taking her nipple between his teeth and teasing it with his tongue. He then dipped said tongue into her navel, then circled her prize, marking the territory he was about to explore. Chey's back arched of its own volition. Her legs spread. It was as if her body resorted to reacting solely on instinct. Her mind was too preoccupied, being overtaken by the intense yearning for this man. Hunter parted her lower lips and tested her heat level, dipping into her carnal volcano and then gently gnawing on her bud. Chey rolled her hips, matching the rhythm he strummed. He devoured her until she shook ferociously and grabbed his ears. She shrieked his name while her juices flowed like lava.

Chey felt as though she were floating back to earth from the cosmos. Hunter excused himself quickly and returned sheathed. He kissed her kitten before entering her slowly and deliberately. Chey gasped, grabbing handfuls of her blanket when he'd filled her. Her neck stretched to its limit as her head lolled back and her back arched firmly. Together they rocked until they could hardly stand each other's fiery touches. His head rolled, as did his eyes when ecstasy took his body under siege. She wrapped her inner walls around him snugly, not wanting this to end. He exploded. Groaned. Bucked. Shuddered and finally collapsed into a panting heap.

Hunter pulled her back to his chest, covered them with the additional blanket. They held each other until her lids became too heavy to continue watching the embers dance in the fireplace.

Chapter 11

Hunter hadn't intended to make love to Chey, but that was exactly what had happened and he didn't regret one single second of it. He couldn't possibly consider what they had indulged in to be merely sex. Hunter had skillfully taken his time with her, checked in frequently to make sure that she experienced the satisfaction she deserved and worked to ensure that she reached euphoria. From the way her body writhed and squeezed and her vocals quivered, he was sure that he'd exceeded his intent. Her moans were music to his ears and he'd strum whatever it was that generated her uttering just so he could hear the beautiful sound. He felt the need to handle her with care and dignity, hoping to make her feel like his priority.

Hunter had been pleasantly and pleasurably surprised when he reached his own peak. His body had convulsed violently in a way that he'd never experienced before. It was as if Chey had sparked an addiction and each time after the first, he'd yearned to reach that same core-clenching, body-quivering high from the previous romp. And he had, reaching and surpassing sensations that made his eyes roll back and left him spent.

Even now, hours after their third or fourth romp, as they lay naked under several covers in the belly of the dark night, Hunter woke up reminiscing. With his arms still wrapped snuggly around her torso, he could feel the rhythm of her breath on his arm as she slept. Remembering the sweet scent they'd created made his jewel stiffen against her backside. If he didn't rein his thoughts in, he'd become hard as a diamond. Not wanting to disturb her peaceful sleep, he adjusted himself and then got up, covering himself with one of the blankets.

As Hunter walked through the cold, dark villa, illuminated only by the light of the moon, he thought about the fact that there was a good chance that he'd never see Chey again. He couldn't understand why he was so drawn to her. Hadn't he just gotten to a point in his life where he was no longer interested in indulging in meaningless trysts? Despite how reality stacked up against this notion, he couldn't help feeling as though this was more than a tryst.

Outside, Hunter could see that the power still hadn't been restored. His eyes closed in frustration and he let the hand that he used to peek through the window fall hopelessly to his side. Maybe the outage wouldn't affect his chances of getting to the airport. He had to make that flight. Rubbing the goose bumps that now covered his arms, Hunter felt his way through the spotty darkness and threw another log in the fire. He needed to use them sparingly.

Hunter slid back under the covers, molding his body against Chey's. She stirred in his arms, found a new position and settled back into her sleep. Hunter smiled when she ruffled the quiet with her light snore.

Hunter recalled the stories about her hometown in Virginia. He'd never believed in the viability of long-distance relationships, but perhaps Chey could be worth trying one out. He needed to find a way to make this last longer than just one night.

Chey was a refreshing departure from his usual cast of eligible women. She hadn't once referred to any of her shoes or garments by their labels. Her boots were just her boots and her coat was simply her coat—none of that "my Prada shoes" or "my Louis Vuitton handbag" talk. She was unapologetically who she was. Grounded. Confident. Beautiful. Fun. In fact, he wondered if she truly realized how beautiful she was since it seemed like no big deal to her. Some of the women in his past all but added their beauty to their résumés, as if it were an accomplishment that they should continuously be praised for—should a man ever forget.

As the firsts hints of day began to peek over the mountaintops, Hunter nudged Chey. The sight of the moon yielding to the superior light of the sun was too majestic for her to miss.

Chey stirred again, finally opening her eyes at Hunter's insistence. Blinking and focusing, she looked up at him and smiled. He smiled back. Angling his head to the side, he motioned for her to look toward the window. Together they sat up and watched the day take over the night.

"Thanks." Chey smiled. "That was beautiful."

With Chey's body cradled in front of Hunter's, they sat watching nature's show until the chill in the room became too much to bear on their naked skin. Rather than put on clothes, Hunter threw more wood in the fire and drew their makeshift bed closer to the fireplace. Pulling her back to his chest, Hunter wrapped his arms around her once again and felt heat rise in his groin. He caressed her hardening nipples, made trails down her torso and dipped his finger into her wet, heated cave. Chey's head fell back against his chest and she maneuvered her hips, giving Hunter more access.

Hunter licked his finger and turned her around for a direct taste. Burying his face between her thighs, he took her pearl between his teeth and determined that she was as succulent as, if not more than, he remembered. He had come to know her body during his intense study hours before and quickly had her singing a melody of pleasure that ended with bravado. He pulled himself away, slipped on a condom and entered her with an urgency that nearly blinded him. She met him thrust for thrust until her second release of the morning spilled over him, making the ride a bit slicker. Hunter held her hips as if he were holding on for life.

"Oh...Hunter!"

Chey's body shook. Hunter's thrusts grew more intense. She encouraged him not to stop in a sweet whisper that took Hunter over the edge. That delicious shudder racked his body. He pumped harder, trying not to be overtaken by the immense pleasure. He was determined to love on her until the last possible second. Losing control of his ability to maneuver, Hunter's body convulsed hard. Spasms shot through his muscles. His back stiffened like a board. A groan started in his core, rumbled through his chest and released from his mouth, and at the same time, he pulled away and released life in spurts, stretching his erection to its limit before melting into a sated pile on top of Chey. She wrapped her arms around him and held him tight. Being in her arms felt good.

They lay for a while, holding each other as the sun slowly continued its ascent.

"I hope you have no regrets." Hunter spoke first, rising on his elbow. He traced triangles between her breasts and navel.

"None." Chey took a deep breath before continuing. "You're going home today...hopefully, right?"

A solemn moment passed.

Another beat thumped in the silence before Hunter responded. "Yeah."

"We shouldn't sound so excited about this," she teased.

Hunter chuckled. The moment labored on, heavy with things that were left unsaid.

"I guess I need to get my stuff together and work on getting to the airport before that plane takes off without me."

"Yeah." Chey avoided his eyes.

The fire crackled. Hunter's fingers still traced shapes on her torso. It seemed that neither of them wanted to break up what they'd started, but no one wanted to say too much.

"We should definitely exchange—"

Chey put her fingers to his lips. "Don't!" Hunter blinked a few times. "I'm a big girl," Chey continued. "I knew what I was doing. I enjoyed it and will remember you for the rest of my life. Please don't ruin this by making promises you won't keep. All I want you to know is that I'm not the kind of girl that does things like this all of the time. You may not believe it but this is my first one-night stand ever and although being with you was amazing, I'm pretty sure it will be my last."

This was a first. No woman had ever shut him down this way before. Hunter couldn't think of a reply that wouldn't sound like an empty promise, so he kept his mouth closed. For several moments, they sat in awkward silence. Hunter looked down upon Chey, who avoided his direct gaze. With a soft touch, he turned her face toward him. They stared at each other, pondering but not speaking until Hunter closed his eyes and kissed her soft and slow as if he was trying to embed the feel of her lips into his long-term memory.

Chey wrapped her arms around his neck. Hunter held

his body over hers and desire sizzled between them. Taking his time, Hunter kissed her and then pulled himself up. He reached for protection, sheathed himself and entered her slowly. His thrusts were sensually rhythmic and intentional, almost desperate, like a sultry blues bass line. Her moans were like crooning, complementing that bass.

As he went deeper, she groped at him as if he were in jeopardy of falling out of her reach. She gripped him, not wanting to let go. He didn't want to be let go of. Neither wanted to reach an end. He savored every second, almost wishing he could slow down time. He made love to her, wanting to leave an imprint on her soul—make it impossible for him to ever be forgotten. When he could no longer stand the delicious, almost torturous pleasure, both burst through the heights of their peaks like rockets shooting through the ozone. Screams erupted throughout the villa, neither of them caring what their neighbors heard. Grappling for each other, they held on tight, riding the wave of delight until they floated back down to earth and reality.

Hardly any words were spoken as Hunter took a cold shower, dressed and got his belongings together for his trip back home. It almost felt unfortunate when the concierge confirmed his ride to the airport. Now that guests were finally able to leave, Hunter also made sure that Chey had been relocated to a villa on the side where the power was working and then paid for her entire stay.

After exchanging reluctant goodbyes and one last dire kiss, Hunter was on his way, hoping she'd hold on to the paper he'd left on the coffee table with his email address and telephone number. In a matter of a few short days, in the midst of an unfortunate circumstance, Chey had managed to stimulate his mind, satisfy his body and stir his emotions. Hunter knew he had to find a way to see her again.

Chapter 12

Chey wondered if she had done the right thing by pushing Hunter away. After seeing him off, she longed for his company. She chided herself for hushing him because she was too scared to hear what he had to say. It was better for her to just agree to the fact that nothing could possibly develop between them. This, she convinced herself, was just an adventure that she would cherish, and soon enough, she'd forget all about Hunter—maybe.

Chey had settled in her new villa on the other side of the resort. Now she was ready for the ski lesson that she was supposed to take days ago. Chey had planned with the intention of enjoying this excursion alone, but now without Hunter, she felt lonely.

"It's time for some action!" She pumped up her attitude. "I didn't come here to mope around. I came for an adventure."

Chey threw on her gear and headed for the slopes. The frigid mountain air had frosted her fingers by the time she reached the lodge. She went straight for the gift shop to purchase a new pair of gloves, some that were better equipped to shield her hands from the bitter cold of the Utah mountains. She stuffed the cute but useless gloves that she'd come with inside her bag and met up with her instructor—an older gentleman with messy salt-and-pepper hair that hung over his eyes and skin that suggested he'd spent much more time on the sand than in the snow.

After being with her instructor, Casper, for an hour and a half, she'd been called a cute little snow bunny too many times to remember, ridden the magic carpet, face-planted a time or two and had at least one yard sale. Becoming familiar with the lingo, she didn't mind being called a snow bunny, the name she'd earned because her outfit was cute and not necessarily effective for ski attire. And she wasn't ashamed to admit that she had more fun riding the magic carpet, or ski lift—especially after face-planting a few times, which meant falling on her face. Her grand finale was the yard sale, or rather, the fall that sent her skis, poles and one of her boots flying in different directions.

Chey returned to the villa sore from her lesson, limping and laughing at herself and Casper's wild sense of humor. After peeling off her cold wet clothes, she stepped into the hot shower, and along with the water, thoughts of Hunter came raining down on her. She wondered if he'd made it home. Where was home, exactly? As much as they'd talked, they hadn't shared much personal information. She'd shied away from that as much as possible. All she really knew about Hunter besides the fact that he was a skillful lover was that he was also a lawyer and he had brothers. Chey had kept the exchange of personal information to a strategic minimum. She'd seen the note he'd left with his number and email address on it. Without reading thoroughly, she'd tossed it in her suitcase but had also thought about tossing it in the trash.

Chey stepped out of the shower and her stomach rumbled. She dressed quickly and headed to the concierge to find a restaurant off the grounds for a good meal and maybe a little shopping. The concierge called her a taxi, which took her to a small downtown area with shops and restaurants owned by locals. After filling her belly with one of the best burgers she'd ever tasted from what looked like a sketchy dive but had come highly recommended, she filled a few bags with souvenirs for herself, her sister and her parents.

Chey's trip was finally turning into the one she'd intended, until nightfall, when memories of her time with Hunter met her in front of the fireplace. She closed her eyes and felt his presence, smelled his masculine scent and remembered the sound of his husky whisper as he checked in to make sure he was loving her right. She didn't miss just his physical presence; she missed him, period.

A moan escaped Chey's throat. A shiver radiated from her core. She sat straight up and looked around. Despite being alone, she cleared her throat and repositioned herself in the chair.

"Damn you, Hunter!"

Chey got up, found her cell phone and went to the bedroom for her suitcase. Flipping the top back, she rummaged through her clothes but stopped, huffed and rolled her eyes before slapping it closed. Chey plopped on the bed with her arms folded in front of her and clucked her tongue. She couldn't be the first to call, but she hadn't given him her information.

"Ugh!" Chey flopped back on the bed. If she called him, she had to have a reason. That made sense to her. When she couldn't come up with a reason that sounded sane, she marched back to the living room and folded herself comfortably on the couch and dialed Deanna.

"Hey, snowbird! How's the trip going?"

"It's snow bunny, and it's going fine." Chey laughed. "I went skiing today," she sang.

"Oh my goodness! How was it?"

"Painful!" Chey had Deanna laughing hard as she recounted her first attempt and many blunders.

"Sounds like you're done with that."

"Not at all!"

"Really, Chey?"

"Despite the fact that my hip feels like it displaced itself, I had fun. I want to get better at it."

"If you insist. How's Hunter?" Deanna teased.

"Hunter should be home."

"Aw. He left?"

"Wait! Deanna. What happened to 'I can't believe you let that stranger sleep in your villa'? And when did we get to being sad about him leaving?"

"I was enjoying the updates. You know I'm living my adventures vicariously through you right now. What a disappointment!" She laughed. "Do you miss him?"

"Actually…yes!"

"Oh! Do you like him? He *was* gorgeous."

"Deanna, why do you sound like a twelve-year-old?" Chey shook her head.

"Ha! I kind of feel like one. Now, tell me, did you start liking him once you got to know him a little? I don't know if I could have stayed in that room with a man as fine as him without getting into at least a little bit of trouble."

Chey cleared her throat.

"Chey."

Chey swallowed.

"Chey!"

She pursed her lips and looked around as if she were avoiding eye contact with Deanna via the phone.

"Oh. My. Goodness! Chey! You did it with that man!" Deanna's scream pierced Chey's ears and her laugh filled the line. "Say it!"

"Um…" Chey tried her best to suppress her smile, knowing it would burst into full laughter.

"You can't lie to me." Deanna spoke the truth. Chey never could lie to her older sister.

Instead of answering, Chey burst out laughing. "Okay! Okay!"

Deanna screamed again. Chey pulled the phone from her ear and shook her head.

"Just tell me…was it good?" Deanna shrieked. Chey imagined her standing with her fist to her mouth in eager anticipation of her response. She made her wait a beat.

"Mind-blowing and body-shuddering good!"

"Whoo! I can't believe it, sis. Who knew that when you set out on an adventure, it would turn out like this? I couldn't have called it. I can't believe it!"

"Neither could I." Chey laughed and then fell silent for a moment as she contemplated asking her sister if she should call to make sure he'd gotten in. "I was thinking…"

After a long bout of silence, Deanna nudged Chey. "About…"

"It's just that I was wondering if he'd gotten in safely."

"Did you guys exchange contact information?"

"Not really…"

"Uh…"

"He left his information. I didn't give him mine. I feel a little funny about calling."

"Text him!" Deanna said as if it were the most obvious solution.

Chey drew in a deep breath and let it out slowly. "I'll think about it."

Chey got off the phone and thought about texting him for the next few hours. Later she sat before her computer and started working on her novel. She opened her email program and stared at the word *Compose*. She figured, if anything, email was less personal than texting and it would keep Hunter from having her cell phone number.

Chey remembered the refined yet sultry masculine manner in which Hunter carried himself and again imagined the type of woman he was probably used to. Surely they were as gorgeous as he was, with judges, doctors or lawyers as parents—like him. They were clearly not the offspring of struggling small-town shop owners. Todd's family had done well, but they were country folk, not big-city savvy at all. Hunter was experienced in a way that differed from the way she'd grown up.

Somewhere between working on a new chapter and getting another cup of hot cocoa, she mustered up enough courage to open up a new-message template on her computer. With fingers hovering over the keys, she deliberated over what she should write. *Keep it simple.* Chey lifted her hands from the keys and let them fall in her lap. Blinking toward the ceiling, she deliberated some more.

"Okay!" she said to the air as her fingers raced across the keyboard, tapping out an almost formal memo. She deleted that and tried again, repeating this action several times. Finally, she settled on something a little less formal but certainly not personal enough to reflect how intimately they had come to know each other.

Dear Hunter,
It was great meeting you. I just wanted to check in and make sure you made it back safely. Take care.
Chey.

Swirling her finger over the laptop's mouse pad, she took several moments before finally clicking Send. Then she sat back and exhaled.

Deciding that she'd had enough adventure for one day, Chey fired up her iPad, pulled up a movie on Netflix and watched until her eyes were too heavy to stay open. In her dreams, Hunter met her at the fireplace.

Chapter 13

Hunter rushed off the elevator at his office with a bagel stuffed in his mouth while balancing a cup of coffee, a newspaper and his briefcase in his hands. Greeting his staff with a raised elbow, Hunter nodded a few hellos, as well. Blake was on the phone as Hunter walked past his office. Inclining his head, he summoned his receptionist, Rona, who despite her tender years, acted more like the firm's den mother. She scurried from her seat and met him at his office door.

"Goodness, Hunter," Rona chided, grabbing the coffee cup and newspaper dangling from his hand. "Let me get that."

Hunter took the bagel out of his mouth, "Thanks." He unsteadily set his briefcase down on the desk. Rona disappeared and returned immediately with a coaster for his coffee, a notepad and a pen.

"Do you need a moment before we start?" She caught the briefcase before it tumbled to the floor, dropping her pen and pad in the process. "Settle down and eat your breakfast. I'll be back in ten minutes. Let me know if you need anything."

Hunter plopped in his chair and acknowledged her with a nod. Allowing the chair to absorb the weight of his morning, Hunter rested his head back and breathed, taking in his first unrushed moment in the past twenty-four hours.

Hunter thought back to the cautious trip through the icy mountain roads that had almost made him miss his flight. All through his security check-in, he could hear his name being summoned for last call. He'd run through the maze of travelers at the crowded airport, leaping over people lying on the floor using their luggage as pillows, and made it to the gate just seconds before it closed. He'd snaked his way through the airplane, reminded of the fact that he'd booked too late to get a first-class ticket. He'd folded himself into the narrow seat, his long legs strained against the chair in front of him. He was forced to endure that uncomfortable position for two whole hours as the plane sat on the tarmac getting its wings deiced. Sheer fatigue and three servings of scotch had helped him sleep through the rest of his turbulent five-hour flight.

This morning his quandary had continued when he slept through his alarm, waking when he should have been walking into the office. Now as he sat in his chair, he let his mind flow back to yesterday morning when he said goodbye to Chey in the most intimate way. Those thoughts generated a slight response in his pants but were interrupted by a knock on his door. Hunter looked up to Blake walking into his office with a familiar grin—one that often had an interesting story behind it.

"What?" Hunter's shoulders slumped.

"Ha!" Blake sat in one of the chairs in front of Hunter's desk and rested his fingers under his chin in the shape of a steeple. Hunter raised his brows. "I got a few calls from Tricia," Blake said.

Hunter's hands instinctively flew to his temples. "Tricia. Yeah. I need to speak with her."

"She was freaking out because she hadn't heard from you."

"Yeah." Hunter had to handle that situation. It annoyed him that she'd called Blake. "I'm sorry, man. How did she even get your number?"

"She called the office. Then she kept calling to 'check on' you. She was concerned about your safety because she couldn't get in contact with you directly."

Hunter had all but forgotten about Tricia. Consumed with Chey even now, he hadn't thought to call one time now that he was home.

Blake rose and walked around to Hunter. "I haven't even welcomed you back, brother." Their embrace ended with a pat on the back from Blake. "Glad you finally made it out of the tundra!" Blake's laugh thundered throughout the office, giving Hunter his first hearty one for the day.

Blake returned to the chair in front of Hunter's desk and filled him in on their current cases. Rona joined them and reviewed his schedule for the rest of the week. Despite his fatigue, Hunter remained rather productive. He called and spoke to his parents for a while. Then it was time to tackle the one task that he'd been avoiding for most of the morning—emails. Hunter pulled up both his work and personal email accounts and when his eyes landed on Chey's name, next to a message with no subject, he smiled as he reminisced.

In spite of the brevity of the email, he paid close attention to every detail, noting the time she'd sent it the night before. He was still in the air when she'd hit the send button. After the best of the most selfless lovemaking he could remember and teetering on the edge of an emotional connection, this was all she had to say? Hunter didn't know if he was annoyed or disappointed. *What's wrong with me?* His conscience shook him back to reality. He'd just met the woman. It was…what it was—an amazing one-night-and-the-next-morning stand!

However, Hunter was back at home and it was time to focus on real life. He plunked out an equally cool and distant response thanking her, letting her know that it was great meeting her, as well, and that he'd finally gotten home safely. He tapped Send and sat back. The tone of the email wasn't unlike that of one he'd send to a colleague. Moreover, that stony '*Take care*' that she'd sealed the email with felt like a dismissal—the final note on a sad song.

Hunter shook his head, wondering what had come over him. He had a stream of women to choose from—many of whom were just as beautiful…maybe. At the very least they were certainly more accessible.

Hunter looked at his watch and decided to take an early lunch and shake off the feeling that he couldn't quite label. He was still somewhere between annoyed and disappointed but now also added rejected to the mix.

After putting his laptop to sleep, he straightened out the brief he'd been reviewing and placed the documents in a neat pile. As he stood, Rona appeared in his doorway.

"Mr. Barrington." He looked at her curiously. She always called him Hunter unless there were clients present. "There's someone here to see you."

She stepped aside and Tricia stepped into view. Her lips were twisted in a playfully chiding smile. "Well, hello, Mr. Barrington."

Hunter narrowed his eyes ever so slightly. Rona's back straightened. She'd gotten the message. "Hello, Tricia." He remained professional.

"She insisted on surprising you, Mr. Barrington. I advised her that I was required to announce all guests." Rona briefly cut her eyes at Tricia and directed her attention back to Hunter. "But she followed me anyway."

Hunter sniffed out a small chuckle. "Thanks, Rona. It's fine."

"See, I told you!" Tricia victoriously stepped around Rona with her nose practically scraping the ceiling and sauntered toward Hunter. Walking around the desk to his side, Tricia placed her hand on the lapel of his suit jacket. "I was so worried about you." She looked back at Rona, sporting a cunning smile. Rona rolled her eyes and walked off.

Hunter hadn't missed her feline-like territorial claim. Moving her hand from his lapel, he responded, "Sorry to worry you. The past few days have been…trying." He patted his pocket to make sure he had his wallet. "I'm glad you're here. Do you have time for lunch?" She grinned and he could have sworn he heard purring. From the way she stood, he knew that she was expecting a kiss. "We need to talk."

Tricia stiffened, her body settling into a more rigid stance, a vast contrast from the flirty position she held seconds before. Hunter headed for the door and, like the gentleman that he was, stepped aside, gesturing for her to go through first. Tricia appeared to be fastened to the spot where she stood. It took a moment for her to start toward the door. Clearly, she understood the message in his cool tone, which didn't match her sultry one. Lifting her head, she stepped out with Hunter following closely behind.

Lunch was as unpleasant as he'd expected but necessary. Tricia couldn't understand why Hunter wasn't interested in seeing her anymore and no explanation seemed to suffice. Hunter tried to express himself in the most honest and cordial manner possible. Still, she left in a huff, demanding that he lose her number.

An hour later she called him, apologizing for her behavior and requesting they get together at her house for dinner and to "just talk." When Hunter told her that he didn't think that was a good idea, she tossed him a few choice words and sealed her irritation by hanging up before he could respond.

Now with Chey in the distance and Tricia out of his life, he turned to focus on the big case in front of him and the email with the details of an opportunity that he'd been pining after. Thanks to his frat brother Eric and his connections, Hunter was being offered a chance to work as a visiting professor of business law at Dunford University.

Hunter had been born into a family whose DNA was laced with an innate desire to give back, and teaching was his preferred way of serving his community. The ability to instruct students at his alma mater made this opportunity all the more incredible.

In the email, Kenya Davis, a professor on the tenure track and Eric's childhood friend, advised him that the opportunity had just become available, the university was impressed with his credentials, and if all went well this semester, there was a good chance that they would offer him a position starting in the fall, replacing a professor who had just made an abrupt departure. For Hunter, pressure was exhilarating since he was confident that he was up for the task.

Maybe the excitement of this big break would keep the random thoughts of Chey that taunted him and brought warmth to several parts of his body at bay.

Chapter 14

After taking more lessons with Casper and finally getting all the right gear, Chey found herself falling in love with winter activities. By the time she left Utah, she had snowboarded and even ventured off the bunny slopes. Without the distraction of Hunter's sensual presence, she'd written a few more chapters in her book and made a few acquaintances at the lodge and in town.

Now she was back home and had given Deanna her complete account of the entire trip. Chey was ready to shift her focus to starting school and finding an additional part-time job to help with her expenses. She couldn't help but sing the encouraging lyrics of "Fly" along with Nicki Minaj and Rihanna. Just like them, she'd come to New York to win. Chey danced and mouthed the words as she got dressed. She was heading to a building in Midtown that housed one of New York's largest cosmetic giants to apply for the position of customer service representative. This position offered flexible hours and weekend work and would fit perfectly into her schedule with school and her current part-time job as a receptionist.

When she had tweaked the last few strands of her

short mane into place and was satisfied with her look, she grabbed the handbag her mother had given her as a gift before she left. It was large enough to fit a laptop and sleek enough to pull off the polished professional look she wanted to achieve.

Stepping out of her tiny abode and onto the snow-covered city streets, Chey still pinched herself at the notion of living in New York. She was glad to finish things she'd started so long ago and applauded herself for being brave enough to go for what she wanted without looking back. She was proud of the hard work that she'd put in to help her parents get their store back on track and save enough money to make the move and go back to school.

It was her time, she thought as she strutted to the subway, effortlessly dodging the throngs of people on the street and feeling like a real New Yorker. When she'd first arrived, Chey couldn't believe how many people were out at all times of the day and night. In all her years, she hadn't seen that many people in one place at one time unless there was a fair in town. She'd awkwardly navigated the crowded sidewalks like an amateur, clumsily bumping people and apologizing. A time or two, she'd been turned completely around by folks whizzing by in rush-hour haste.

Now she strolled as though she'd been living there all her life, blending in like a native. Chey made it downtown to her interview with a half hour to spare. Settling in at the coffee shop across the street, she ordered a chai, sat and read her book for a while. When it was time, she boldly crossed the wide street along with a multitude of other unfazed pedestrians as the noses of turning cars drew perilously close. She'd grown accustomed to the precarious dance between vehicles and pedestrians as the swift rhythm of the city pulsed in her gait.

As she walked inside the building, a male frame in

a gray suit caught her attention in her peripheral vision. Chey turned her head and saw a man with an uncanny resemblance to Hunter walk into a building a few doors down. She stopped walking and someone bumped into the back of her.

"Oh! I'm sorry," she said. The person, undeterred, circled around her and kept walking without missing a beat.

Chey looked back at the door she thought she'd seen Hunter walk through, dismissed the notion and continued into the building. She found her way to the reception desk and announced her purpose. Moments later a young woman with a smart bun, black dress and ballet flats escorted her to a conference room, where she awaited the arrival of the hiring manager.

The interview went swiftly, leaving Chey with a sinking feeling that she might not have aced it as she'd planned. The aloof woman stood and cracked a hint of a smile as she shook Chey's hand and let her know that she'd be in touch. The bubble she'd sailed in on had been burst, and that left her questioning how well she'd come across to the hiring manager.

Still reeling from her interview, Chey fell into step with the barrage of city folk and turned into a small sushi restaurant a few doors away. By the time her food arrived, Deanna was calling. Chey told her about her interview but not about the possibility of seeing Hunter. Deanna bid her good luck and ended the call. Chey sat for a while eating and reading until she looked up and saw that same masculine frame covered in a well-fitting gray suit standing near the hostess. She craned her neck to get a better look but could see only the back of him. Just like Hunter, he was tall, brown and handsome even from behind.

Chey's heart rate quickened from the possibility of being in such close proximity to Hunter once again. She couldn't move from her seat. Would he remember her? Would he acknowledge her? Why hadn't she considered the possibility that he could be from New York? He certainly had a Northern accent, absent of the lilt of Southern tongues.

Chey watched intently from behind her menu as the hostess approached him again. He began to turn and stopped. Chey's heart paused. Now she could almost see the side of his face. What would she do? He turned a little more, but not enough for her to see his full profile. Her heart started back up to a full thumping that she could feel on the outside of her chest. Should she get up? Should she stay? If she left now, she'd have to walk right past him.

Why was she so wound up? The hostess gestured for him to follow her and he did, turning around. Chey set her eyes on the menu, refusing to look up. She couldn't stand the anticipation, so she looked up in time to stare right into his face. He smiled at her, a handsome, inviting smile. It wasn't Hunter. Chey tried to stop her heart from pounding. She looked down at her barely touched food and summoned the waitress.

"I'd like to take this to go." She pointed to her plate. The waitress nodded and went away. Chey gathered her things.

When the waitress returned with her check and container, Chey quickly dumped the rest of her food inside, dropped her money on the table and headed for the door. When she looked back, Hunter's slightly less gorgeous doppelgänger looked up. Chey turned and left.

Chey hiked a full block before stopping to take a breath. Her heart was still racing. What had just happened? Then she truthfully answered her own question as she continued down the street at a more reasonable pace. She couldn't face Hunter. What would he really think of her? As much as she'd enjoyed throwing caution to the curb and indulging in several blissful romps with him, she found security in the fact that she would probably never see him again. What decent girl had sex with a stranger after knowing him for just two days? Despite her honestly telling him that it was the first time in her life that she'd ever done something like that, what were the chances that he believed her? A man like him must have heard that crap as often as *hello*.

Chey headed home and prepared herself for the start of classes the next day. As much as she wanted to forget about her encounter, she couldn't get Hunter out of her mind. Despite the amazing things he'd done to her body, she thought about how they could never make it in a relationship. *Relationship! What's wrong with me?*

Chey reached for the teakettle. A cup of chamomile would help settle her thoughts. The afternoon was young. She plopped onto her secondhand couch, folded her legs under her bottom and sparked up her laptop. Her plan was to spend the afternoon writing. Once classes started, she assumed she wouldn't have much time to write.

Chey had reached the part of the book where sexual tension sizzled between the hero and heroine like lightning. The kettle shrieked, jolting her from her fictional world. She fixed a cup and returned to the couch. Images of her and Hunter bathed in darkness, dimly lit by the fire's embers, played across her mind and she typed out every stimulating detail she could recall from their searing encounter. By the time she finished writing, the sun had retreated for the night and she had missed her prime-time shows. Warmth radiated from her insides. Her pearl had awakened and longed for Hunter's touch. She shut down her computer, took a cool shower and went to bed with memories of him stroking her thoughts.

Chapter 15

Hunter ended the conversation with his parents and headed out of his office in a rush. Classes started today, and after his brief meeting with Kenya the day before, he was even more excited. All day he wondered about his syllabus, his students and how his classes would go. Kenya had confirmed that what he had planned for the students during this semester was both valuable and innovative. Adrenaline pumped through his veins like water rushing downstream after rainfall.

Kenya was a pretty woman with soft-looking skin and beautiful fluffy coils of hair that sprung from her head in a wild yet polished fashion. Though she was attractive, Hunter looked forward to getting to know her as a colleague and friend. He wasn't one to mix business with pleasure. He left that trap to his younger brothers.

Trotting down the subway stairs, Hunter hit the platform with pep in his gait. The train screeched to a halt and the doors opened right in front of him. He stepped aside to avoid being trampled when a thick batch of riders came pouring out. It didn't even bother him when one passenger who'd just realized that he needed to get off pushed past him, almost knocking his briefcase from his hands. Hunter sighed and plugged his ears with the music streaming from the playlist on his phone. Bobbing his head as he held the pole, he swayed with the train as it tumbled through the stations.

A rush of cold winter air made Hunter pull his coat tighter as he ascended the stairs on the Upper East Side neighborhood of New York City. He arrived at school early enough to find his classroom before going to set up his temporary office.

"You made it?" Hunter looked up to find Kenya standing in the entrance to his office. Her voice sounded lower than it had in recent conversations. She leaned on the door frame and folded her arms in front of her.

"Hey. Yes, I did." Hunter clapped his hands and rubbed his palms together. "I wanted to get an early start."

"Good! Want me to walk you over to your classroom?"

"Actually, I just came from there. I know exactly where it is."

"Well—" Kenya smiled "—I'll leave you to finish setting up. My office is just down the hall if you need me."

"Thanks! And again, I can't thank you enough for helping with this opportunity."

"It didn't take much effort at all. Your credentials are quite impressive. The university prides itself on the fact that they have working professionals teaching cutting-edge curriculum."

Hunter appreciated her comment. "Thanks."

"What you can thank me for," Kenya started, snatching Hunter's full attention, "is my recommendation that you be considered for the board."

"Pardon me!" Had Hunter heard her right? "You recommended me for the board?"

"There's a vacancy on the board of trustees and I mentioned your name. A few of them liked the idea."

"There are faculty members on your board of trustees?"

"You're looking at one of them."

Hunter nodded, impressed. "So now there's more riding on this than I thought."

"Just act like you didn't know if someone approaches you about it, okay?"

Hunter held up three fingers like a Boy Scout. "You have my word. Thanks again."

"You're welcome." Kenya smiled and turned.

Assuming she was leaving, Hunter turned his attention to his briefcase. He pulled out some pens and placed them in an empty drawer.

"Perhaps you can thank me for the board recommendation by taking me to dinner."

Hunter looked up. He stifled a laugh. It was obvious that she was coming on to him. "You choose the place." His voice dipped lower than he had intended. His eyes scanned her slim waist and curvy hips before reaching her face again. The playboy in him was practically instinctive, able to be strummed to the surface without much coaxing. He remembered that he wanted to date with more of a purpose these days. Despite the fact that she had a pretty face and nice curves, she was a colleague and a potential fellow board member. That could become messy very quickly. He'd promised himself that he'd keep things on a friendly basis to avoid the kind of confusion screwing a coworker could inflame.

"Are you busy today after class?"

"Actually, no."

"It's a date, then." She cast her eyes upward. "Well, not an official girlfriend-boyfriend kind of date, but it's... How about I just say it's confirmed." She laughed.

"Consider it…confirmed," he teased.

As he watched her walk away from his office, Chey came to mind. Why? He didn't know, but he allowed the reminders of her supple skin and sensual whimpers to entertain him while he prepared for class. When he glanced at the clock, it was time to go. Kenya met him in the hallway on the way. Her next class was a few doors down from his.

A few students were already inside his classroom when he arrived. Since he had a few more minutes before starting, he stood outside the room and continued to talk to Kenya, who was giving him some more basic information about the culture of the university. A few students excused themselves, passing between Kenya and him to enter the classroom. As the room filled, nervous energy swirled inside Hunter, but no one would ever have been able to see past his confident facade. Strong poker faces were also a part of the Barringtons' makeup.

Hunter looked at his watch. It was time to start, but Kenya didn't seem to want to stop talking. He excused himself politely by asking where she wanted to meet after class.

"Oh. How about your office?"

"That's fine! See you."

Leaving Kenya, Hunter stepped inside a classroom full of fresh newly adult faces, sprinkled with a few more mature ones. Assuredly, he strutted toward the desk at the front of the class, acknowledging several people with polite nods. Placing his briefcase down, he sat on the side of the desk with one foot still planted on the floor and scanned the entire room. That was when his ability to maintain the Barrington poker face failed him.

His eyes met the shocked expression on Chey's face and he suddenly felt as if the air had been siphoned from the room in one swift motion.

Chapter 16

A few students who looked as though they had just reached the legal voting age walked into the classroom snickering about how good-looking the new professor was. Some stood aside blatantly gawking at him through the opened classroom door. Chey giggled, remembering when she was that green fresh-faced college student. Now that she was twenty-seven, she felt like the elder in the classroom.

At first, Chey thought it was the cute stranger from the sushi bar. Second, she thought her imagination had forgotten its place in reality and played tricks on her. At last, she realized that neither of her initial notions was correct and her mouth fell open at the sight of Hunter walking in and taking an authoritative stance in front of her classroom. Hunter—the same Hunter whom she'd thought she'd never see again—stood before her in the flesh. From the look on his face, Chey sensed that he was just as shocked as she was.

The room grew deathly quiet and curious stares bounced back and forth between the two of them. Hunter was the first to snap out of their confounded trance. He cleared his throat and addressed the class with his rich, deep voice.

"Good evening, class. My name is Hunter Barrington, and I will be your business law professor for this semester."

With the fluidity, grace and confidence of a male runway model, he floated to the board and wrote his full name.

Chey swallowed the obstruction lodged in her throat as she tried to recover. She pulled out her schedule and looked at the names of her professors. Barrington was listed. Instantly, a picture of him introducing himself by his full name back in Utah unfolded in her mind. Chey put her hand on her head. She needed this class to graduate in May, but how would she survive?

Chey looked up. Hunter was still speaking, but she hadn't been focusing on the words coming out of his mouth. She was too busy vacillating between thoughts of dropping the class and thoughts of Hunter's chiseled naked body. She knew exactly what was under that tailored blue pin-striped suit.

Chey yearned to get up and leave but didn't want to draw any attention. She'd have to suffer through this one class, but first thing tomorrow morning, she was going to meet with her advisor to change her schedule. She pulled out her iPad, attached the keyboard and pretended to pay attention. As hard as she tried, she couldn't focus. That was proof that she needed to change classes. There was no way she'd pass when she couldn't concentrate on anything that came out of the professor's luscious mouth. The same mouth that had had her reaching pitches that she'd thought her vocal cords were incapable of attaining. The same plump, smoldering lips that had set her skin ablaze with hungry kisses and a long tongue that…

"Huh?" Chey pulled her head out of the sexually charged recollection. "Did you call me?"

"Yes. Ms. Rodgers!" Hunter blinked those long lashes

at her. A hint of a knowing smile curled at the ends of those lips.

"Uh…yes?"

Hunter smiled, and Chey felt her stomach flutter.

"I was taking attendance." Hunter raised a brow.

"Oh…um…here." Snickers erupted from some of the fresh-faced students—men and women. *How embarrassing!*

"Gordon Smith?" Hunter continued calling the roll.

Chey got up and headed for the door.

"Ms. Rodgers?"

"Just going to the bathroom," she said without turning back.

Chey scurried through the hall in search of the nearest ladies' room, burst through the door, rested her hands on the sink and took several breaths. Then she laughed. Loud. Chey laughed until the sound of her laughter filled every crevice of the bathroom and bounced off the sterile walls. She doubled over and held her stomach and then leaned back and let the laughter roar until tears streamed from her eyes.

"Only me," she said to her reflection between chortles. "Something like this can only happen to someone like me!" Tittering, she wiped her eyes and peered into the mirror. "Chey Rodgers, what luck you have! I'm screwed!" The pun sent Chey into another fit of snickers. "Whew. Okay, get it together, Chey!" She splashed water on her face and wiped with a paper towel. "You can do this." She stood straight, lifted her chin and drew in a sharp breath before walking out of the bathroom.

Chey tiptoed quietly back into the classroom and took her seat. Although the class was only an hour and a half, it felt as though time refused to move. Concentration was a challenge, but she did manage to take a few notes. When the end finally came, she dashed to the door, but Hunter called her name before she could make a clean exit.

Chey paused, swallowed and turned around as gracefully as she could. *What does he want?* She turned to acknowledge him with a forced cordial smile. Hunter nodded at students as they said their goodbyes. When all had exited, he walked over to her. The thump of his shoes permeated the empty classroom, or was that her heartbeat?

"Hello," Hunter said, his cavernous voice all but melting her resolve. She remembered the sound of that voice bellowing, whispering in her ear.

"Hello, Hunter." Chey cleared her throat.

"I never imagined—"

"I know!" She shook her head. The irony of this situation made her laugh. "Never in a million years."

Silence swelled in between each of their comments, making the conversation seem labored. The start of each sentence was almost jarring.

Hunter curled that lip up into a handsome smile and chuckled. "Never." His eyes burned through her for a moment. "So you live in New York? Who would have thought?"

"Yeah, East Side." Chey wanted to look away but found it hard to do so. His striking features commanded her attention. He stared directly in her eyes and she could see desire behind the surprise. "Oh. Um…thank you for taking care of my room bill. That was so unexpected."

"Thanks for taking me in." He stared at her for a moment. "We should do dinner sometime."

"Sure." She didn't know what else to say but was sure that there were probably some rules against student-teacher dinners and she couldn't risk losing her partial scholarship due to inappropriate behavior. "Do you teach other classes?"

"I hope to. For now, just this one on Tuesdays and Thursdays."

"Oh…okay?"

"Yep," Hunter added after a while.

Quiet invaded their space again. Chey averted her eyes, unable to stand his intense gaze any longer. His eyes never left her.

"Um…" she began. "I should be going. It was…interesting…seeing you again."

That elicited another chuckle from Hunter. "Tell me about it."

"Well…take care." Chey turned to leave and Hunter reached for her arm. Something stirred and radiated from the point of contact down to her fingers. She looked at his arm to make sure it wasn't glowing with radioactive energy. He let her go.

"Dinner," he said matter-of-factly. It wasn't a question. "Are you free tonight? It would be great to catch up."

"Oh! Um…sorry. Tonight won't work," she lied. *Neither will ever!* Chey shook her head, donning her best regretful expression, hoping it worked. Hunter looked genuinely disappointed. She took a breath. *Might as well take care of this now.* "I had a great time in Utah, but…usually… Fact is, I've never done that kind of thing before. I'm not good at casual dating… I've got a lot on my plate right now and—" Hunter chuckled again. Chey stopped speaking and narrowed her eyes. She wasn't sure what was so funny and tried to rein in the anger that was rising in her.

"Now I understand." He laughed a little harder.

"Understand what?" Chey's response was curt. Her scrutinizing gaze turned her eyes into thin slits.

"When I look at you, I see a beautiful woman who made an adult decision to do what she wanted and liked it, so she did it again. Nothing more. Nothing less. No judgment here." Hunter held up his hands.

Chey's cheeks burned with embarrassment. Hunter saw right through her. Either he understood how she felt or he had bedded so many women within days of knowing them that their time together hadn't fazed him one bit.

"It's just that—"

Hunter held his hand up, stopping her midsentence. "The woman I met in Utah," he said referring to her, "was interesting, fun and a person that I'd like to get to know better. I'll admit I was shocked to see you in here but glad at the same time. I've wondered about you." Hunter paused. Chey fidgeted. "So about that dinner."

"Aren't there rules about dating students?"

"I'm sure there are, but I didn't ask you on a date. I asked if you would like to have dinner."

"So it's not a date?" Chey inclined her head sideways.

"No!" Hunter challenged her with his raised brows and a pearly white smile.

Chey didn't respond right away. She hadn't got to know anyone else in the city yet and thought it would be nice to get to know someone, even if it was Hunter. Chey continued to ponder her decision. Changing classes would also put her at a safer distance.

"Have dinner with me. Don't worry. I'll still respect you in the morning. Ha!" Hunter teased and his laughter exploded throughout the classroom.

Chey swatted his arm. "Very funny." She was still a little embarrassed, but Hunter was doing a good job of making her feel better about their tryst in Utah. "Okay. I'll let you take me to dinner."

"Does Thursday work? We can go right after class, and if you're up for it, maybe a little game of Spit or I De-clare War."

"Oh!" Now Chey really laughed, reminiscing about their game day in Salt Lake City. "Yeah! Only if you promise not to cheat!"

"I didn't cheat last time. I won fair and square!" Hunter held both hands up innocently. Generally amused, they reminisced for a moment, laughing and recalling funny memories. Being in his presence felt familiar again. Their laughter was interrupted by Professor Davis entering the room with a curious gaze.

"Hey!" She looked between Chey and Hunter. "Hunter." She nodded. "Ms. Rodgers." She nodded in Chey's direction. "You two know each other?" She wagged her finger back and forth between them.

Chey remained quiet, not sure how to answer. Professor Davis assessed her from head to toe and then raised her chin like a feline raising its back in defense. Chey sensed that she was being territorial.

"Yes," Hunter finally said.

Kenya's eyes volleyed back and forth as if she was waiting for more. When it was clear that no one was offering any more details, she faced Hunter, turning her back to Chey.

"I went to your office looking for you. Are you ready to go to dinner?" she all but purred. It was as if Chey had suddenly become invisible. She almost shivered from the coolness that emanated off Professor Davis in her direction.

Chey inclined her head and stretched her eyes at Hunter. *Dinner?* Without allowing another beat to pass, she turned and headed for the door.

"Nice chatting with you, Professor Barrington." She hoped that he could sense the bite in her remark. How dare he ask her to dinner? It was pretty obvious there was something between him and Professor Davis. Chey had initially pegged him correctly. He was a player and there was no way she was getting caught in his web, no matter how gorgeous he looked or how great he was in bed. Right then she wondered if he had slept with Professor Davis, as well, and she was immediately aware of her own sense of jealousy.

"See you Thursday, Ms. Rodgers."

Hunter's words hit her back. Chey now had two classes to reschedule. She wanted out of Hunter's and Professor Davis's classes.

Chapter 17

Hunter and Chey had talked for hours while cooped up in the villa. They'd covered a lot of ground, yet so much about her remained a mystery. He knew plenty about her early years in her small town in Virginia, her fond childhood memories and her appreciation for simple things like great movie classics and fun games. However, what intrigued him most were things she hadn't said—the subjects that had been broached but left uncharted.

Today he realized that it was much more than unfulfilled curiosities that drew him in, keeping thoughts of her at the forefront of his mind. Hunter liked her raw beauty, her presence, her smile, the way she dipped her shoulders and threw her head back when she laughed—those, among other more explicit things. Hunter simply liked Chey.

Now he also understood why she'd been so cold when he was leaving and in her email. She was concerned about him respecting her after their delectable heated encounter. She was simply being defensive. If only she knew the Barrington brothers were experienced—to put it nicely. They knew the difference between women with standards and those who indulged in one-night stands with the same casual flair as they chose a pair of shoes to go with a certain outfit.

He'd received his student roster days ago but hadn't paid enough attention to it to notice her name. When Chey practically ran out of his classroom after Kenya showed up, he'd calmly resisted the urge to run after her. He hadn't missed the way Kenya planted herself between the two of them and then touched him as if that were their norm. He'd remained stoic because there was too much on the line. Unlike his brothers, he wasn't up for being "the talk."

Dinner with Kenya had seemed like a fine idea until the woman who plagued his dreams reappeared in his life. Now as he sat across the table from Kenya as she boasted of her credentials, he couldn't keep his mind from wandering back to the moment he'd recognized Chey sitting in his class. Time had stopped. No one else was in the room but Chey and Hunter. His mouth had watered and his jewel had stiffened at the sight of her and the memory of her sweet taste. Hunter couldn't recall being this affected by another woman. Not even the woman he'd dated throughout law school and briefly thought about marrying.

Politely, Hunter continued to listen to Kenya drone on about her upcoming sabbatical and spending the summer traipsing through Southeast Asia. By any standard, Kenya was an intelligent and experienced woman who would be quite the catch for any man. Right now Chey held his mind hostage. He wondered what she was doing now. Who was she with? Where exactly did she live?

"Hunter!"

"Yeah." Hunter furrowed his brows, pretending to listen intently.

"Did you hear anything I just said?" Kenya was clearly on the verge of becoming annoyed. "You seem rather preoccupied."

"I'm sorry. I have a lot on my mind."

Kenya smiled, obviously accepting Hunter's mild lie. Taking a carrot from the crudités plate, she dipped it in the dressing and slowly brought it to her mouth, stopping short of taking a bite. "What are you thinking about?"

"I wouldn't bore you with the details." Hunter stabbed a piece of steak and stuffed it in his mouth.

"You could never bore me." Kenya bit into her carrot.

"Heh." Hunter appreciated when a woman went after what she wanted, but he hated when the chase was effortless. He connected with Kenya's line of sight, assessed her for a moment and sat back, placing his fork on the side of the plate. "So tell me. What would you like to see happen between us?"

"Wow. Damn the small talk." Kenya reached for her wine. After a healthy gulp, she put the glass down and stared into Hunter's eyes for a tick. "We both have a lot going for us. You look good on paper and in person."

Hunter resisted the urge to roll his eyes—something he didn't normally do, but if he had a chip of gold for every time a woman considered how attractive his credentials were, he'd have enough gold to fill all the vaults in the Federal Reserve twice. At one time, that would have piqued his interest—made him push out his chest a little. Right now he wasn't impressed.

Hunter wasn't interested in making a connection that "looked good." He wanted one that felt good, and not just to his extremities.

Hunter leaned toward her. "I've never dated women I've worked with. I've seen that get…'messy.'" He curled his fingers into quotes.

"There's always a first time for everything. Besides…" Kenya took another sip. Hunter assumed the rawness of this conversation was more than she was ready to handle on a sober mind. "I'm a grown, intelligent woman who understands boundaries."

"What would those boundaries look like?" Hunter drew even closer to her. He was interested in hearing how she was going to answer this question.

"I realize we work together. Whatever we decide to do, we set the limits and abide by them, whether we date, have casual sex or a full-blown relationship."

"What kind of connection would you prefer?"

Hunter saw a flash of embarrassment and then a coy smile spread across Kenya's face.

"Well, I don't know." Kenya gestured for the waiter to come and ordered a different drink. No wine this time. She must have needed something stiff. Hunter ordered a scotch. "What kind are you up for?"

Hunter sat back again and smiled. "I asked you first."

"Whew. Well…I guess I'm willing to explore all of those options and see where they take us."

"Aren't there rules against this kind of thing at the university?"

"Those fraternizing rules apply to relationships between students and teachers, not colleagues. In fact, there are one or two married couples who are on staff."

"Interesting." Hunter knew that if he wanted Kenya, he could have her tonight. He'd still respect her in the morning. He found nothing wrong with a forward woman. However, the desire was simply not there. He knew what kept his desire at bay. Her name was Chey. "I'm going to be honest. You're a beautiful woman, brilliant and stimulating." Kenya's fair cheeks turned pink.

"But…I can hear it coming." Kenya picked up the drink the waiter had just placed on the table, swirled the ice with the stirrer and sipped.

Hunter chuckled. "I'm looking forward to getting to

know you more as a colleague first. I think we'd make great friends. Besides—" Hunter took a breath "—as far as relationships are concerned, right now I'm in an… interesting place."

"What's her name?" Kenya raised a brow.

Hunter tossed back the remnants of his near-empty snifter and picked up the fresh one that the waiter had just placed on the table. "The name isn't important. It's more like…" Hunter searched the ceiling for the right word "…timing. I like being clear about my intentions and I'd never want to mislead you."

"Good ole Mr. Time." Kenya nodded. She placed her hand on his. "I appreciate your candor." Kenya motioned for the waiter. Hunter sensed that dinner was over. "You can't blame a girl for trying. Maybe in time…*timing* will no longer be an issue."

Hunter just smiled. *Maybe.* Right now time was the only thing that seemed to stand in the way of exploring something deeper with Chey. He'd find a way to work that out.

Chapter 18

The past two days had come and gone too fast. Now Chey stood just inside the building chatting with her parents to avoid going to class early. As if she didn't have enough to be embarrassed about, she'd made things worse by wearing her jealousy on her sleeve and storming out of Hunter's class the other day. She had spoken to her advisor about getting her schedule changed, but the courses she needed weren't being offered at other times. Besides, she had already picked the most convenient schedule possible. Three classes were held on Tuesday and Thursday with a break between the second and third—Kenya's and Hunter's. The other two were on Monday, Wednesday and Friday evenings.

Kenya had watched her intently during today's session and Chey hoped she wouldn't become a problem. She looked at her watch and realized she had only minutes to spare before Hunter's class started.

"Hey, parents!" Ray and Patricia were on the speakerphone at the store and were going on about how much the customers loved the new lotion she'd created before she left. "Mom. Dad."

"Yes, sweetie?" Patricia finally opened up the conversation enough to allow her to get a word in.

"I may come home during one of our long weekends. I can make more then."

"That would be great!" Patricia said. "I still don't like the idea of you being out there in that city by yourself. I don't see why you had to pick a school in New York. There are plenty of schools here in Virginia."

"Ma!"

"Sounds like a plan," Ray added, heading off a potential bickering session between Chey and her mother. "Hey. Why don't you whip up something for the men, too, while you're here?"

Chey knew that her dad was equally concerned, but he seemed a little more supportive.

"Okay, I'll look into that. I have to run now. Class starts—" she looked at her phone for the time "—now! Love you. Bye!" Chey ended the call and raced down the hall.

She reached the door just as Hunter was about to close it. He smiled at her. Not a "welcome to class" smile either. His luscious lips curled into a sexy grin that shimmied up to his brown eyes. She looked away.

"Good afternoon, Professor Barrington." She held her composure and took the seat closest to the door. After the tingling sensation settled down, she remembered that she should have been more irritated than affected. He shouldn't give her looks like that when he obviously had something going on with Professor Davis.

Again Chey found it hard to concentrate in class, but she did better than the first day. She even took more notes. This time, they were actually more coherent, as opposed to being random snatches of information typed across her screen. She still couldn't bring herself to participate further or raise her hand, even though she knew the answers. The less Hunter looked her way, the easier it was to get through the class. She had already caught him staring a few times.

Chey kept looking at her watch, counting the minutes until class finally ended. After shutting down her iPad, Chey leaned over to place it in her bag. As she came up, she saw Hunter's legs in front of her. Her breath caught. She rose slowly.

"Hey!"

"Can we talk?" Hunter asked.

She wanted to say no, but he summoned a yes from her with those irresistible eyes and that strong jawline.

"Let's go to my office."

Chey stood. "Lead the way."

Just as they stepped out of the classroom door, Professor Davis walked up.

"Chey," she delivered curtly with a singular nod. Then her voice changed. "Hey, Hunter! Have you eaten?" She looked at him as if she wanted to have him for dinner.

"No, but I'm fine. I need to speak with Ms. Rodgers for a moment and then I'll be heading straight home. I have court in the morning and this judge can be a piranha."

"Oh. Okay." Kenya responded to Hunter but her eyes were on Chey.

"Can I give you a call after court? I have a few questions," Hunter said.

"Sure."

"Great! Take care," Hunter said.

The walk to Hunter's office felt awkward since Kenya trailed them by a few steps. Hunter touched on the subjects they had just discussed in class. Chey was sure that was for Kenya's benefit because when she turned into her office on the right, Hunter stopped speaking as they continued toward his office a few more feet to the left. He didn't start speaking again until they were behind the closed door in his small office.

Chey stood by the door as Hunter rounded his desk. When he sat, he looked up and gestured toward the seat in front of him.

"Please. Have a seat. Get comfortable."

Chey sat.

For a moment, he just stared at her. A slight smile teased the ends of his lips.

"What, Professor?" Chey tilted her head sideways.

"Hunter." Chey watched his lips move as he spoke.

"What, Hunter? Why are you staring at me like that?"

"I don't mean to make you uncomfortable."

"Well…" Chey let the idea hang and gave him a look letting him know that he was doing just what he hadn't meant to do.

Hunter laughed. Chey didn't know why, but she joined him anyway. The oddity of the situation was still funny no matter how awkward it felt.

"I still can't believe this." Hunter slapped his desk.

"You! I thought I would have a heart attack when I saw you walk into that classroom."

Chey was pleasantly amazed at how easily they fell into a familiar rhythm now that they were alone.

"I wanted to speak with you since Tuesday, but other than your email, I don't have any of your contact information." Chey didn't offer any details. Hunter continued. "How was the rest of your trip? Did you ever get to go skiing?"

"Did I!" Chey opened up and told him about her days in Utah after his departure.

"Sounds like things went well. I'm glad the storm didn't ruin all of your plans. Did you work on your book?"

If Chey hadn't been smitten by Hunter at this point,

he'd have won her with that last question. No one seemed to care about her desire to write—least of all her last boyfriend. And here Hunter was, asking about it as if he truly wanted to know.

"Actually, I made a lot of headway on it. I really like how the story is coming along."

"You'll have to let me read it one day."

"It's romance." Chey waved him off. "You won't be interested."

"Why wouldn't I be—especially if you're the one writing it? Do you have someone to proofread it for you?"

"No." Chey couldn't believe his level of interest. Todd would have never offered to read her book.

"Maybe I could do that for you." Hunter sat back in his chair and put his hands behind his head.

Chey chuckled. "Wow. You would do that?" It was a nice gesture, but she'd never let him read it—especially with all the steamy details that were inspired by him.

"Of course." Hunter leaned forward. "Did you put anything about me in there?" He flashed a curious gaze paired with a wicked smile.

Chey shook her head. "Hunter!" she admonished. Her cheeks burned again.

He laughed. "Just curious. Maybe you should." He paused and returned to that intense gazing that he always laid on her. Chey squirmed a little. His eyes were so passionate. Another moment passed before he started again. He leaned forward, taking on a more serious presence. "The reason I asked you in here was to break the ice a little. In class I noticed you seemed uneasy." Chey nodded, confirming his notion. "In Utah you mentioned finishing school. Is this your final semester?"

"Yes. I have five classes and then I can graduate." Saying those words brought back the excitement of being close to accomplishing one of her biggest goals. "Two in science and three in business to fulfill my requirements for a business minor."

"Great! Therefore, I assume you'll want to ace my class."

Chey twisted her lips at Hunter. "I've always been a great learner." Chey could tell by the way Hunter's eyes dipped and sparkled with mischief that he had received her statement with the naughtiest of intentions. "Hunter!" she chided once again. "I'll never survive this class if you keep doing that."

"Ha! Okay. I'll behave. I don't have much of a choice now, do I?" Both laughed at that. "On a more serious note, I have a bit of a situation."

"What's that?" Chey asked, feeling even more comfortable.

"I really want to get to know you better, but obviously, under the circumstances there are…limitations."

Chey swallowed.

"Really."

"Yes, really." He stared at her incredulously. "This university has very strict rules against professors 'fraternizing' with students." Hunter reached into his drawer and pulled out a thick spiral-bound book with the university's logo on the cover and plunked it on the desk. Chey stretched her eyes in disbelief. "Now, being an attorney, I read through it looking for the loopholes."

Chey laughed. "Are you kidding me?"

"Not at all! Whoever wrote this handbook did pretty well, so it basically renders you off-limits to me, but it doesn't say anything about being friends. So as a friend, who enjoys eating, I'd like to invite you to eat with me tomorrow evening around eight."

Chey's shoulders shook as she tried to contain her laugh. "You're serious, aren't you?"

"There are certain things I don't play around with." The look on his face conveyed the gravity of his words.

Chey stopped laughing. "So a friendly dinner, like the one you had the other night with Professor Davis," she said matter-of-factly. Hunter tilted his head at her jab. "Okay. That wasn't fair." She drew in a strident breath, pondering his proposal, and then let it out slowly. "I don't know, Hunter. Besides, I don't get out of class until eight." Internally, she questioned the viability of this "friendship." "There's a lot on the line here. This can get touchy."

"Only if we let it." Hunter winked. "We can do dinner at nine-thirty to give you some time after class." Chey shook her head and sighed. He rose from the chair, came around and sat on the desk. "Look." His tone turned serious again. He had Chey's full attention. "I realize we both have a lot at stake. Teaching here at my alma mater is something I've always wanted to do. If I do well this semester, it can lead to a permanent position and a possible consideration to join the board of trustees. This is an amazing opportunity for me. You've waited a long time to finally finish school. I can tell this means a lot to you by the way your eyes brighten when you talk about it. Despite that, I've wanted to know more about you ever since I left Utah. I accepted that it couldn't happen, until you showed up in my classroom. If the closest I can get to you is being your friend, I'll take it. This doesn't mean you don't have to do your best in class." Chey's head snapped toward Hunter. He smiled and Chey knew he was teasing her with that last statement. "So how about it?" He stretched his hand toward her for a shake. "Friends?"

"Friends." Chey shook his hand and once again electricity sizzled through her when they touched. The roguish look that gleamed in his eyes showed that he'd felt it, too. Chey looked at her watch. "I'd better get going." Slowly, she pulled away the hand that he was still holding.

The knock on his door startled them both.

"Come in." Hunter beckoned, walking back to his side of the desk.

In walked Professor Davis, surveying the place as if she was trying to decipher what had happened in there. Her eyes skittered between Chey and Hunter, examining their faces as if she might be able to read what they might have been hiding. "You're still here, I see." She smiled at Hunter but slightly tapered her eyes at Chey.

"Just leaving now." Hunter grabbed his briefcase and motioned for Chey to walk ahead of him. "Take care, Ms. Rodgers, and don't forget what we talked about. I believe you'll do just fine this semester."

"Thanks, Professor. I'm sure I will," she said cheerfully before offering Kenya a forced smile.

"Take care, Ms. Rodgers." Kenya's acknowledgment was terse.

Chey knew Kenya could be a problem.

Chapter 19

"Who is she?" Blake parked himself at Hunter's desk and interrogated him with his glare. Hunter moved his head left, then right. Blake followed, never breaking his eye contact. "What's her name, bro?"

"Ha!" Hunter shook his head. "Who are you talking about?" Clueless as to what had brought on Blake's line of questioning, Hunter flipped open his laptop, practically dismissing his brother and his crazy inquiries.

"You walked in here singing this morning. Didn't you notice?"

Hunter reared his head back, scrunching his face at Blake incredulously. "No, I didn't."

"Uh! Yes, you did. Does this look familiar?" Blake rose, went to Hunter's door and two-stepped back toward his desk singing 'You Got What I Need.'"

Laughter bubbled from Hunter's gut. Blake had his mannerism down pat. "I did that?"

"And apparently, you hadn't even noticed. So spit it out!"

Besides discussing their current caseload, Hunter and Blake had hardly spoken this week. Hunter filled Blake in on the details about Kenya, Chey living in New York and being one of his students, and the obvious jealous tension emanating from Kenya.

"Whoa! You have to be careful with that one." Blake referred to Kenya. "Women can be tricky when they have a thing for a man."

"That's why I asked what her intentions were and let her know where I stood." Hunter sat back confidently.

"You're a Barrington. I don't have to tell you how much drama a woman can bring even when she supposedly knows her lane. Plus you left a window open, man." Blake sighed.

"A window?"

"You presented a loophole! Women take loopholes and create craters. Just be careful. Make sure your colleague truly comprehends where you stand. Don't do it right away. If it appears that she hasn't gotten the full picture, you may have to paint it for her again."

"How!" Hunter scrunched his face at Blake. "I told her exactly where I stood."

"You told her the issue was timing—therefore, she's going to hang around and wait for the right 'time' to make her move. As far as she may see it, you didn't shut her down completely. You set her aside. You may have been better off telling her you were already involved with someone."

Hunter pondered Blake's comment for a moment, then wiped his hand down his face. His legal mind connected the dots. "You're right." He leaned over his desk closer to Blake. "Yesterday after class, I told Chey to come to my office so I could talk to her. We were in there for a while. Next thing you know, Kenya comes knocking on my door. I thought she'd left the building already." He sat back, rubbing his chin.

"She wanted to see what was going on. I wouldn't be surprised if she was standing outside trying to hear what you had to say. Tread carefully, brother. Some women can be worse than men when they set their sights on something they want. You're finally accomplishing goals that you've sought to do for a long time. It would be a shame if someone got in the way of that. Keep your eye on the prize."

Hunter stared down at Blake. "Pot calling…"

"I know…the kettle. Believe me, I know what it's like to feel like you've hit the jackpot with a woman and your mission to break the bank sets itself in motion before you realize it."

"Huh?" Hunter's confusion showed up in his etched brows and upturned lip.

"Ha! Basically, I knew there was something special about Cadence and I went after her hard."

"Got you! You were falling for Cadence before you actually realized your feelings were so strong. What's with the riddles?" Hunter chuckled and Blake shrugged. "Who said I was going after Chey hard?"

"Have we met?" Blake looked around as if his surroundings were unfamiliar. "Dude! I'm your brother. I know you better than anyone."

Hunter wanted to deny that he was already smitten with Chey. In fact, he had been since he'd spent those few incredible days with her in Salt Lake City. "Pfft!" He dismissed Blake's claim with an unconvincing wave. "I'm just checking her out."

"And you felt the need to break things off with that fine honey Tricia? You're throwing Kenya to the back burner. Since when haven't you been able to focus on more than one woman at the same time? You've cleared house, Hunter! You've made room for this woman in your life already."

Hunter was quiet. He didn't want to confirm or deny anything, yet Blake's assessment was one hundred percent true.

Blake shook his head "Uh-huh. You don't have to admit it, bro. I know what I see. The same thing happened to me." Blake rose. "Keep on denying it. I can't wait to meet her so I can say 'I told you so.' Ha! If I were a different kind of man, I'd put money on it."

Hunter could only watch as Blake began strutting out of his office. He picked up a pen and tossed it at him as he reached the door.

Blake sidestepped the assault and continued strutting until he cleared the office. Once outside, he popped his head back in. "Have fun 'eating' tonight, because it's not a date, right? Ha!" Blake disappeared with his boisterous laugh wading in his wake.

Hunter still couldn't put a finger on whatever it was that drew him into Chey's world. What he did know was that the mere thought of Chey brought on an avalanche of sensations—ones that piqued his interest and certain parts of his anatomy. Could it be that he just wanted more of her physically? He dismissed that notion. At the end of the day, sex was sex; he was drawn to much more than Chey's body. His thoughts weren't frequently hijacked by memories of her just because she was great in bed—or on the floor in front of the fireplace.

Glancing at the beautifully crafted clock, Hunter shifted his focus. He needed to be in the courtroom in an hour to face Judge Piranha. She'd earned that name for figuratively biting off the heads of a few young overzealous attorneys in her time. Cockiness was a no-no in her presence. That old woman, who was years beyond retirement age, was a barracuda who didn't bother hiding her distaste for arrogant attorneys. Fortunately, Hunter was a Barrington man and handling women, both young and old, was a skill they'd mastered early in life. With a little humility, a few compliments and some subtle flirting, he seemed to stay on her good side. However, if she ever sensed that he was being disingenuous, she wouldn't hesitate to bite his head off, too.

Eric was calling as he stepped out of the subway.

"What's up, man?" He greeted his frat brother with a smile in his voice.

"It's all good. How's the teaching gig?"

"So far, so good?"

"What do you think about Kenya?"

"She seems nice."

"Yeah. She's not a shy one." Eric chuckled.

"I found that out. Ha!"

"She's just…what should I say…progressive when it comes to her perspective on sex and dating. Reminds me of a man, sometimes."

"Has she always been like that?"

"Pretty much."

Hunter stopped just outside at the base of the courthouse steps, suddenly pensive. "Have you ever tapped that?"

"A real man never kisses and tells." Eric didn't deny or confirm Hunter's question.

"Yeah! You just told me all I needed to know." Hunter laughed. In his mind, Kenya was now completely off-limits. "I'll holler at you later."

"Cool!"

Hunter ended the call and jogged up the stairs. Just before entering the courthouse, he remembered that he hadn't spoken to Chey to confirm their dinner that night.

Hunter snapped his fingers. All he had was her email. He'd meant to get her number the evening before while they were in his office, but then Kenya had shown up. He wasn't going to ask for Chey's contact information in front of her. He could have gotten it from the school records but preferred Chey to give it willingly. Hunter searched his emails for the memo he'd received from her when he'd left Utah. He touched Reply and tapped out an email confirming their dinner plans and requesting her address and contact information. He shut off the phone and headed to his designated courtroom.

Inside, Hunter was focused on his case but couldn't wait to get out and check his phone. He kept wondering if Chey had emailed him back. A couple hours later, when the judged banged her gavel, Hunter made a swift dash for the door. Opening up her email felt like opening a present. He held his breath as he read, hoping she didn't attempt to cancel. He needed to be with her off school grounds and out of Kenya's reach.

An easy smile spread across his face and he put his phone away. It was time to find out more about Chey and figure out what it was about her that held his thoughts captive.

Chapter 20

Chey couldn't remember being so nervous. She paced as she considered several outfits that were strewn across the full-size bed in her small bedroom—a black long-sleeved sweater dress that she planned to pair with boots, jeans with a black turtleneck, another pair of jeans with a pink cashmere sweater and printed leggings with a long sweater that would cover her round bottom.

"It's not a date," she chanted as if she needed reminding. "We're just going out to eat." That motivated her to remove the dress. Besides, it could come across too sexy because of the way it poured over her curves. Then she ruled out the turtleneck because she didn't want to look like a walking chastity belt. Hunter had already tasted the fruit. Who was she fooling? She picked the jeans and pink sweater and opted for brown boots.

Chey gasped when she looked at the digital clock on the table next to her bed. The green numbers taunted her. Since she'd gotten home from school, she had spent too much time yapping with her sister and then trying to figure out what to wear.

Within the next fifteen minutes, Chey had showered and

slathered on one of her favorite silky creations, and she left the room smelling like vanilla lilies. She stood in front of the mirror and fingered her short curls in place. She hated rushing, but since this wasn't *a date*, she didn't have to work so hard at trying to be impressive. The buzzer rang as she applied liner to her eyes and lips. In a few short steps, she was looking over Hunter's head from her window. He even looked good from the top. His tall frame stood perfectly erect. Once again a small fire burst in her belly.

"This is not a date!" Chey cleared her throat as she ran to the intercom. "Hi, Hunter. Come on up. I'm on the fourth floor." She pressed the button to listen to his response just in time to hear the end of *okay*. When she turned around, she wished she hadn't invited him up.

Her tiny apartment, which was usually tidy, still had breakfast dishes in the sink. A pile of mail sat on the coffee table. The shoes she'd unevenly stepped out of were spread across the floor, and her bed, which could be seen from the living room, was still covered with the clothes she'd decided not to wear.

Chey picked up the shoes and tossed them across the room, almost knocking down her lamp. She grabbed the mail, placed the frying pan from this morning in the sink with the rest of the dishes and dashed to her bedroom to close the door just as she heard a knock on her door. Chey looked around to see if she needed to move or hide anything else.

Drawing in a deep breath, she rubbed her clammy hands down the front of her pants. "Coming." With one last look around, she opened the door. *Damn!* She hoped that she hadn't said that aloud.

Hunter's tall frame filled her doorway, looking like a brown god draped in leather. His freshly trimmed hair and goatee framed perfectly structured features. Come-and-kiss-me lips spread into a sexy smile that revealed a perfect set of teeth that looked more like freshwater pearls.

"Can I come in?" Hunter's words snapped her out of her temporary trance.

"Oh…sure." She stepped aside, waving him in. "Please, have a seat." Chey motioned toward the chair she wanted him to sit in. The couch was much too troublesome to rise from. "I'll just need a few more minutes. Would you like something to drink?" She was already making her way to the kitchen. Her mouth was as dry as if she'd been eating cotton. She needed a sip of water herself.

"Water would be fine."

Seconds later Chey returned with two chilled bottles of spring water. She waited for Hunter to finish removing his coat, scarf and gloves and then handed one to him. His kelly-green shirt fit well, outlining his taut chest. A picture of his bare abs flickered across her mind.

Chey cleared her throat, turned on her heel and headed for the bathroom. "I'll be right back."

Inside, she looked in the mirror and shook her head at her own reflection. She'd seen him in suits at school, bulky jeans and sweaters in Salt Lake City, but today, in those jeans and with that stylish shirt straining against his muscles, Hunter looked hot!

"This isn't a date," she whispered while spreading pink-tinted gloss across her lips. "We're just going to eat. He's my professor now. That's it, that's all." Chey huffed and assessed her reflection. She wiped gloss from the rim of her lips and tossed the tube in her petite makeup bag. She was ready.

"Where are we going to eat?" Chey asked as she pulled a brown parka from the closet and twirled a pink pashmina around her neck.

"I have several places in mind. What kind of cuisine do you have a feel for?"

"I absolutely love Thai. We don't get much of that in my part of Virginia."

"Then Thai it is, and I've got the perfect spot as long as you can handle a little spice."

"Oh, I can handle the spice." The second those words fell from her lips, she wanted to take them back.

"Yeah." He winked.

"You can really be presumptuous sometimes, Professor," Chey chided him with narrowed eyes.

"Okay! I won't do that anymore." Hunter held his hands up innocently.

"Let's eat." Walking out the door with her stunning professor at her side made her feel adventurous but nervous. What if someone saw them? *This isn't a date*, she told herself once more. They were just two friends sharing a meal. It was true that they had known each other before school started. They were just being reacquainted. She had no reason to feel as though she were doing anything wrong. By the time they made it to Hunter's SUV, she'd completely convinced herself that going out with Hunter—to eat—was perfectly fine.

Being a gentleman, Hunter opened every door they approached, held out her chair and waited for her to sit. Once they were seated, he made several recommendations and offered her the opportunity to order first.

Hunter watched her closely. Chey hoped her constant squirming went unnoticed.

"I see there are a lot of Thai restaurants in this area. In fact, there are several on the same block."

"Yeah." Hunter sat back easily. "This is my favorite place for authentic Thai cuisine. It's the real deal and this is not too far from your apartment."

"I thought we got over here pretty quickly. Where are we?"

"Ninth Avenue and Forty-Sixth Street. The West Side. How long have you been in New York now?" Hunter leaned aside to let the waiter place two glasses of water on the table.

"Just a few months. I moved here in October."

"Have you explored the city much?"

"Not as much as I would have liked to. I did get to Rockefeller Center for the lighting of the tree, checked out a few museums. I look forward to taking in a Broadway show sometime soon. There's so much to do I almost don't know where to start. Besides—" Chey looked down, watching her own hands nervously fold and unfold the napkin in her lap "—some of these things aren't cool to do solo."

"Did you know anyone here before you came?"

Chey glanced up at Hunter's penetrating eyes and looked back down. "No. I came here a lot as a kid. My aunt used to live in Brooklyn. She moved south after she retired several years ago."

"I live in Brooklyn." Hunter leaned forward. Chey almost moved back to give herself space to breathe. "Sounds like you could use a tour guide. New York is too intriguing to go unexplored. We need to get you out."

"That would be nice."

The waiter delivered their appetizers, giving her a short-lived yet much-needed reprieve from his presence. Chey's heart stopped beating when she saw Hunter bow his head to bless his food. *And the man prays.*

"What made you choose Dunford U?" he asked when he was done.

"They're known for churning out some of the country's best perfumers."

"You're really into this, huh?"

"Oh my goodness, yes. I've been doing it for years, but I want to be official." Chey told him about her desire to work for Estelle London and one day have her own company.

"That's fascinating. I don't think I've ever met a perfumer before. Are you wearing another one of your creations now?"

"Yes." Chey raised her hand to him. "Smell."

Hunter sniffed. "Hmm. Nice. I want you to make something for men."

"My father just said I need to work on a line for men."

"Smart man."

The waiter came to take away her half-eaten appetizer and deposited a steaming plate of red curry rice in front of her.

"Oh. This smells delicious." Taking a forkful, Chey now closed her eyes and savored the spicy robust flavor and moaned. "Goodness. This is by far the best Thai food I've ever tasted."

"If you think that's good, I can't wait to take you to my other favorite place, in Brooklyn."

"Can't wait! I haven't been to Brooklyn in years."

Conversation flowed as they enjoyed their meal. Chey made sure to find out every detail that she'd missed from their exchange in the mountains. The two bundled up and braved the icy weather as they walked back to Hunter's SUV.

Their dialogue was still full, fun and energetic until they pulled up to the front of Chey's building. Both sat quietly. Chey glanced sideways at his full lips, imagining them against hers, but this was not a date and he was off-limits.

"Are you busy this weekend?"

"No plans." Chey busied herself, twiddling her fingers to keep her eyes off his lips.

"There are a few things happening in the city. I could check them out and let you know."

"Sure." A few moments passed in silence. "Dinner was great." She put her hands on the door handle, not really wanting to get out. "I guess I better get going."

Hunter pushed his door open. "Let me walk you to the door."

They took their time exiting the car and walking to the door. Chey fiddled with her keys before inserting them. She wasn't ready for the night to end.

Finally pushing the door open, she turned to Hunter. "Good night."

"I'm walking you to your apartment door." Hunter motioned for her to step inside the building.

"Oh!" Chey was thankful that she had him for a few more minutes. Taking her time, she sauntered up the four flights of steps and moseyed to her apartment door. They engaged in small talk along the way. And again, she fiddled with her keys.

Hunter stood close behind her. His scent filled her nose. She turned to say goodbye and he closed in on her, his face centimeters from hers. Her breath caught. He closed his eyes and took in her scent. They swapped the air of that small space.

"I want to kiss you." His voice was low and husky.

"I…" She almost admitted that she'd wanted to feel his lips on hers all night. "I know." Moments passed. Sounds of their breathing filled the charged silence. He was so close. If she tilted upward, her lips would be on his.

"Chey." His whisper resonated in her loins. Her stomach tightened.

"This is not a date…remember." Her voice was soft.

"It was just dinner." His nose grazed hers. His breath caressed her face. Hunter spread the palm of his hand on the door behind her, outlining the space around them. "Are you ready to go inside…alone?"

She sucked her breath before finding her voice. "Not really." She was honest.

Grazing her lips, Hunter didn't kiss her, but the light brush left them sizzling with want. "Then let's go!"

Hunter grabbed her by the hand. Chey didn't protest at all. Bouncing down the steps, she followed him back to the car, exhilarated; her body tingled with a staticky mix of excitement and desire, and her heart thumped. She couldn't help but laugh.

"I'm still not going on a date with you, Professor."

"I didn't ask you to," Hunter said.

Chey had no idea where Hunter was taking her and she didn't care.

Chapter 21

Hunter had spent the past hour driving Chey from one end of Manhattan Island to the other, pointing out land-marks and giving her a brief history lesson on the different neighborhoods. He showed Chey the beauty of the lights on the George Washington Bridge at night, let her feel the pulse of Harlem, witness the affluence of the Upper East Side and hop on a carriage ride through Central Park as they shared a hot dog from one of the city's many street vendors.

After the carriage ride, they jumped back in the SUV, passing stores like Gucci, Louis Vuitton and Hermès. Hunter headed south on Fifth Avenue, continuing his tour along the city's most expensive shopping district. Like a child at a picture show, Chey sat in awe at all the sites and changing neighborhoods.

At Thirty-Fourth Street, Hunter made a right, then rode north for several blocks, passing the world's largest Macy's in Herald Square. Hunter continued to the water, then rode alongside the Hudson River on the West Side Highway, past the Chelsea Piers. Ending the tour down by the East River, Hunter parked the car and walked along South Street so

Chey could get a clear view of the Williamsburg, Manhattan and Brooklyn Bridges.

She looked down at her watch. The sun had tucked itself away before the evening had fully unfolded, but it was now well into the night. "It's really true. This city doesn't sleep." Chey shook her head. "People are out all over the place. Back home, my entire town shuts down around nine thirty. It used to be at eight."

"There's still so much more to see," Hunter boasted.

"Really!" Wonder flashed in her eyes.

"Yeah. We didn't go through Chinatown or Little Italy. There's SoHo, NoHo, Battery Park City, the Meatpacking District."

"Wow. I can't believe I've been living right in the middle of all of this and haven't taken it all in. I need to get out more."

"And you haven't hit the boroughs yet."

"Goodness."

They strolled in silence for a few more minutes before Chey stopped walking. Hunter looked to see what had taken her attention.

"What's up?"

"It's beautiful."

Hunter followed Chey's line of sight to the moonlight wading in the East River under the Brooklyn Bridge. For a moment, he admired the sight along with her.

"You know, this bridge is one of the oldest of its type in the entire country. It took about thirteen years to complete it. Construction was completed in 1883." Chey smiled with her eyes still on the historical structure. Hunter continued. "They used to charge people one penny to walk across the bridge, five cents if you rode a horse, and if you had other animals like sheep, pigs or cows, you had to pay five cents for each one."

Chey marveled at his lesson and laughed. "Could you imagine seeing someone cross the bridge now with some sheep or cows in tow?"

"I know. People protested and it's been free to cross ever since."

"Wow." She turned back toward the bridge. "Such rich history."

Hunter noticed her eyes sparkle under the streetlight. He watched the lean line of her neck as she stared up at the buildings. A smile touched her lips as she took in the scenery. He felt a pang of hunger ball up in his core. He wanted to taste her lips again. *She's off-limits*, he reminded himself.

"I have one more neighborhood to show you before I take you back home."

"Wow. It's almost hard to believe there are still parts of the city that I haven't seen."

"Let's go." Hunter took her by the hand. Immediately, he regretted teasing himself with her touch. The muscle between his thighs stirred. Hunter took a breath and they walked back to the car in silence.

Chey stared out the window, clearly eager to continue taking everything in. Hunter couldn't help but smile at how erect she sat, moving her head side to side trying to see all that they passed. He pointed out a few more landmarks until he made it to his destination.

Chey gasped and then broke out into a fit of laughter. "Where are we?"

"The Village!" Hunter rode around for a few minutes in search of a parking spot. He finally spotted one along Washington Square Park about a block from New York University. He rounded the car, then opened the door on Chey's side and helped her out.

"Are you okay to walk a little more?"

"Sure. I'll sleep well when I get back home."

Taking her hand, Hunter led her toward West Fourth Street. They wound their way through the lively streets, checking out eateries, lounges, tattoo shops and clubs.

Again Chey marveled and sometimes gawked at Mohawks, partially shaved heads, hair colored in all hues, bold piercings and punk-rock and goth-inspired clothing juxtaposed against business suits and casual attire.

"Now I truly see how much of a melting pot New York is."

"What makes you say that?"

"Just looking around." Chey stopped walking and did just that, looked around. "There are so many..." Chey pondered a moment, seemingly thinking of the right word "...flavors of people here in New York and still they all just flow together. Everyone is just doing their own thing, not fazed by anyone else's uniqueness. No matter how much a person stands out, they don't...stand out."

"Yeah?"

Chey chuckled. "Back home if you're different in any way, you stand out like a sore thumb. The people are not as accepting of those who don't settle into a specific mold. There aren't many neighborhoods where you will see a person dressed in a business suit walking down the street totally unfazed by the punk rocker next to them or someone with a body full of piercings. Here it's okay to be whoever you are. That's pretty cool."

"That's New York for you."

"I'm glad I'm here."

Hunter stopped walking. "Me, too." Narrowing his eyes, he licked his lips and started walking again.

Hunter could tell Chey was getting tired. Her droopy eyes made her look sexy and staring into them threatened his composure.

"Ready to go?"

As if on cue, she yawned. "Oh. Sorry."

"No apology necessary. I'm getting tired, too. Let's get you home." Hunter turned back and led the way to the car.

"Thanks, Hunter. This was amazing."

"I'm glad you enjoyed it. Like I said, there's still so much to see. Maybe you'll finally get to that Broadway show."

"That would be great!"

"Oh! Wait!"

Chey flinched, startled by Hunter's sudden outburst. "What?"

"We have to do one more thing before I take you home."

Chey stretched her eyes at him as another series of yawns strung themselves together, proving how tired she was. "My goodness! Excuse me. Maybe we should save that for the next time."

"Next time." Hunter flashed a rascally smile. "So there's going to be a next time."

Chey rolled her eyes and swatted him. "Sure, but no dates."

Hunter held his hands up. "No dates." He laughed, grabbed her and gently pulled her along. "This won't take long. It's on the way back to the car."

At the end of the block, Hunter cut a left and walked to a shop tucked in a small nook along the street.

"Do you like crepes?" he asked Chey.

"Sure." Chey put her hands on her stomach. "But I can't eat another thing."

"You'll just need a taste. We can share. This guy has the best crepes in the city."

"He's open now?" Chey glanced at her watch.

"This is New York, baby."

"Oh. Pfft. Yeah. I forgot." Chey teasingly rolled her eyes.

Hunter stepped up to the window to place his order. A few moments later the slim man was passing his crepe through the opening. Hunter stepped out of the way of the patron behind him and unraveled the crepe.

"Here. Taste." Hunter put the crepe up to Chey's mouth.

Chey bit down and closed her eyes. "Mmm. Oh my goodness." She pulled back as some chocolate dripped on the side of her lip. Before she could get to it, Hunter wiped her mouth with his thumb and licked it. Chey blinked but continued chewing.

Hunter took a bite. "Come on. Let's get to the car," he said as he started walking.

"Wait a minute!" Chey stood in the same spot, not moving.

"What's wrong?" Hunter asked, gnawing on another bite.

"I need another bite." Chey stepped to Hunter, rose to her toes and bit the crepe.

"I thought you couldn't eat another thing," Hunter mocked her.

"Who said that?" Chey snatched the rest of the crepe from Hunter and ran.

Laughing, Hunter ran after her. When he caught up with her, there was only a small piece left.

"Here." Chey lifted the remaining piece toward Hunter's mouth. "You can have the last piece."

Hunter's eyes were glued to hers. He made sure his tongue touched her finger as she fed him the sweet treat. She cleared her throat when his tongue made contact. A dribble of chocolate sauce was smeared on the side of his mouth. Chey wiped it and put that finger in her mouth. For several moments, they were arrested in each other's gazes.

"We better go." Chey finally spoke.

"Yeah. You're tired."

Hunter took her hand and escorted her to the car. She fell asleep on the ride back to her apartment. When they arrived in front of her building, he almost didn't want to interrupt her peaceful slumber. Watching her took him right back to the villa when he'd had the pleasure of witnessing her bare chest rise and fall as she rested in front of the fire.

"Chey." He called her name and had to repeat it several times before she finally stirred.

Chey looked around, sitting up as she stretched. "We're here already." She yawned again. "Sorry I wasn't good company on the ride back."

"You're always good company. Even when you're asleep."

Chey managed a lazy smile.

"I guess this is it. Thanks for such a great time."

"You're welcome." Hunter pushed his door open and rounded the car to her side. "Let me walk you to your door. I promise not to drag you back out this time." He helped her out.

"Humph. I don't think I'd make it back down those steps."

Again Hunter walked her up to her apartment, took the keys from her hand and opened her door for her.

"Thanks," Chey said, standing in the opening.

Hunter gave her the keys and took one step back, trying to rein in the overpowering desire to kiss Chey's lips.

"I guess I'll see you in class on Tuesday." She jiggled her keys but hadn't moved to enter her apartment.

Hunter nodded and at first stayed put, but the hunger chided him, chastised his will and took command. In one step, his hand curled around to the small of her back, pulling her in, and his lips connected with hers. The unbridled passion that had been pent up the entire evening unleashed itself, making it impossible for him to release her. Chey's hands found their way to his neck, massaging and caressing it. They kissed until they were breathless, pulling apart to suck in much-needed air.

"Good night, Professor." Her silky whisper graced Hunter's hearing like a feather.

"This wasn't a date."

"I know." Chey turned around, walked inside and closed the door, leaving Hunter leaning against the wall, tantalized by that small taste.

Chapter 22

Hunter's tour encouraged Chey to get out more, and despite the bitter cold, he made good on his promise to help her explore the city. She'd come to know more about New York in recent weeks than she had in all of her years visiting as a child combined. As one who thoroughly enjoyed a good meal, Chey was particularly elated about the many restaurants. She could go days without indulging in the same kind of cuisine.

Chey also enjoyed becoming more familiar with Hunter. The two had become quite comfortable in each other's company and were on their way to being great friends in spite of the sexual tension that crackled in the atmosphere every time they were alone. Beyond their first evening together, they hadn't even kissed again until last night. Chey had given in to her desire and boldly pulled Hunter in for a toe-bending tongue duel that had left them both gasping for air. Usually, they were mindful enough to keep private encounters to an absolute minimum. At school they also kept their interactions cordial and brief. However, that hadn't kept Kenya from detecting the indubitable chemistry between them.

Now as Chey prepared to walk into her Tuesday afternoon class with Kenya, she braced herself for her professor's increasingly abrasive behavior. At first, Kenya had simply watched her closely. Chey would be engrossed in a classroom assignment and sense Kenya's eyes on her. However, Kenya had recently graduated from simply staring to speaking to her in a terse manner that she didn't use with the other students.

Today was much like the others. Chey walked in and addressed everyone cordially and made only fleeting eye contact with Kenya as she found her way to her seat. She felt Kenya's gaze on her. Ignoring her scrutiny, Chey pulled out her iPad and kept her eyes glued to the screen.

As students continued to filter in, she checked her email. She saw that she had received one from the hiring manager from the interview that she had gone on a few weeks back. Eagerly, she opened the email and scanned the contents quickly. The rejection soiled her mood. They had chosen another candidate. Chey huffed and laid her iPad on the desk with the screen facing down. She needed that job. She'd been practicing financial austerity, but now that she'd had a taste of what New York really had to offer, she wanted to indulge more.

Feeling a little defeated, Chey lifted her head and met Kenya's dissecting glare. Resisting the urge to roll her eyes, she challenged Kenya by not looking away. The two locked eyes until, finally, Kenya turned and addressed the students. Class ensued without any further optical showdowns, but as Chey tried to make a quick, subtle exit, she heard Kenya call her name. Chey wanted to keep walking, acting as if she hadn't heard her.

"I need to speak with you, Ms. Rodgers."

What does she want? Had Chey kept walking, it would

have been obvious that she was ignoring Kenya. Halting, she forced a smile, turned slowly and strode to Kenya's desk.

"What would you like to speak with me about, Professor Davis?"

"Just one moment, please." Kenya's eyes were on the stragglers taking their time to leave the classroom. Making eye contact, Kenya nodded and smiled, her polite way of telling them to keep it moving. When the room was clear, she turned back toward Chey and her fake smile faded.

"Ms. Rodgers. There's something I'm a little concerned about."

"But I've been doing well. My test grades—"

Kenya held her hand up, interrupting Chey. "It has nothing to do with your class work. That's been fine."

Chey inclined her head sideways. "Then what is it?" she inquired, baffled.

Kenya sat down and motioned for Chey to take the seat right beside her desk. "It's about Professor Barrington."

Chey reared her head back and tapered her eyes slightly. "What about Professor Barrington?"

Kenya cleared her throat. "Apparently, you knew Mr. Barrington before. Am I correct?"

"Yes…why?" *And why is it any of your business?* Chey wondered.

"It appears that the two of you are rather…cozy with one another. While I don't have a problem with it, the school does." Chey's heart paused. "You see, Mr. Barrington has a lot on the line. The administration and the board are watching him very closely. He's being considered for a permanent position here at the school, as well as a potential spot on the board. Your…friendship—" Kenya said the word as if it tasted bad "—with the professor has the potential to jeopardize an opportunity that Mr. Barrington has worked so hard to acquire. If you're truly his…

friend, I would strongly suggest you keep your distance. I'm sure you wouldn't want to stand in the way of him getting something that he has worked so hard for, right? He's my friend, too, and I'd hate for your exchanges with him to be misconstrued. You do understand what I'm saying, don't you? Besides—" Kenya looked Chey over as if she was assessing her "—Hunter is pretty well established and has a rather impressive pedigree. Don't you think he's a little—" Kenya tilted her head "—out of your league?"

It took the collective effort of Chey's will and every muscle in her body to keep from shaking in front of Kenya. A ball of angry heat had become inflamed inside her core. She wanted to ask Kenya who she thought she was, but she, too, had a lot on the line. However, despite how upset Kenya's words had made her, she had to comply. Hunter had proved to truly be a great friend and she wouldn't be able to live with herself if she was responsible for ruining such a desired opportunity for him. She also knew that the unmistakable chemistry between them was evident. Chey had no choice but to check her emotions and put distance between her and Hunter.

"Sure. I understand." Chey rose instinctively, ready to be done with this conversation and out of Kenya's sight.

Kenya called her as she reached the door. "Ms. Rodgers."

"Yes, Professor Davis?" Her tone was professional, clipped. She held her head up, despite feeling as if she wanted to scream.

"Do me a favor and keep this conversation between you and me. I wouldn't want Hunter…I mean Professor Barrington…to worry about the administration and board's scrutiny. He's already dealing with enough pressure."

"Sure." Chey flashed a smile that failed to reach her eyes. Turning, she made a quick exit and continued walking at that same brisk pace until she reached a small coffee shop just beyond the campus's borders. Chey hadn't closed her coat, yet didn't feel the blistering cool air during her traipse across the grounds.

Finding an available chair, Chey dropped her bag and stood on the winding line to order a latte. Still wound up from Kenya's talk, she opted for a tea instead. She took her cup and settled into the comfortable cushions of the chair that she'd reserved. Contemplating the conversation, Chey considered her options. No matter what, the best thing would be to leave Hunter alone.

With one month of classes behind her, she had only two and a half months to go and she would be graduating with her bachelor's degree. Passing with impressive grades meant a lot to her. She would focus on finding that second job and studying and preparing for her commencement activities.

When her break was almost over, Chey threw her empty cup in the garbage, grabbed her bags and headed back to campus. She'd started the day looking forward to seeing Hunter. Now she hoped that for some reason, he'd be absent today.

Chey's wish didn't come true. As she approached the classroom, Hunter's signature scent tormented her nose before his handsome face even came into view. Chey groaned.

"Hey! I have some information for you, so don't run off after class," Hunter said, smiling.

"Sure." Chey continued past him and headed straight for her seat.

Lately, they'd been leaving school together. Hunter would introduce her to a new place to eat or they'd just hang out at one of several coffeehouses before heading home. He would fill her in on what was happening in the legal world or his brothers' latest antics and she'd talk about her family and her post-graduation plans. At his encouragement, she'd even ordered some supplies and started working on a line of lotions and fragrances for men. She loved that he was so supportive of her dreams.

Without seeing his face, Chey sensed the questioning behind his eyes. She hated having to build a wedge between them but had no other choice.

Chey watched Hunter in her peripheral vision. On cue, he looked at his watch. It was time to start. Hunter peered down the hallway in both directions, stepped in and closed the door behind him.

"Good evening, everyone. Let's get this party started." This ritual elicited a few chuckles every time. Hunter led the class in his usual engaging style, making complex scenarios seem simple.

When class was over, Chey was the first one through the door. Hunter had to practically run out of the room to catch up with her. He grasped her arm. Chey turned around to Hunter panting slightly.

"I have something for you." Hunter craned his head, placing himself in her line of sight as she tried to avoid his eyes. "What's wrong?" Hunter looked around, smiled, nodded and waved at a few students and then turned his attention back to Chey. "Come to my office."

Hunter started walking toward the classroom but stopped and turned back when he realized Chey wasn't following him. She hadn't moved from her spot.

"Chey." Hunter's expression showed he searched for understanding.

"Um…I really need to go. Can you just email me the information?"

Hunter's face twisted in confusion. "What? Yeah. Sure."

Chey headed down the hall and didn't look back. Hunter

had brought so much light to her life. Being in a big city by herself, she didn't mind being alone, but never had she actually felt alone...until now.

Chapter 23

By the time Hunter reached his office, Kenya was leaning against his door.

"Hungry?"

"Sure." It was obvious that he wouldn't be eating with Chey this evening. He hadn't eaten since lunch and was famished. "Let me get my things." Hunter went into the room to retrieve his bags and then walked with Kenya to her office."

"How's class going?"

"Good so far. The students seem engaged."

"That's because they have an engaging professor. I've been hearing great things. The administration seems pleased."

Hunter smiled. Chey's behavior had left him confounded, but Kenya's comment was the catalyst he needed to shift his mood. He'd call Chey later to find out how she was doing. Something had to be wrong.

Kenya and Hunter headed to a nearby bistro and were fortunate enough to be seated almost immediately. They talked about their classes until their meals arrived.

"How long have you known Chey Rodgers?"

Hunter stopped chewing the piece of Chilean sea bass he'd just tossed in his mouth. What was up with the sudden shift in the conversation?

"Just a few weeks."

"Oh!" Kenya sipped her wine. "How did you meet?"

Hunter stuffed a forkful of fish and risotto in his mouth and chewed slowly. "By happenstance."

"Oh!"

Both the conversation and dinner had been going well until Kenya started asking probing questions. Chey was the last thing he wanted to discuss with Kenya. He felt protective of Chey. It was obvious that Kenya wasn't fond of her.

"How are your classes going?" he asked Kenya, taking in another forkful.

"Well." Kenya cut her chicken, but her eyes stayed on Hunter. "So it looks like one of the classmates has a thing for Chey." She averted her eyes. "She's a pretty girl...in a simple kind of way. It seems that a few students have had their eyes on her. She's become rather friendly with one of them in particular. They seem to have made a connection."

Hunter wasn't going there with Kenya. "So I had a meeting with the head of the department. Like you said, he shared that the feedback from students has been great." Hunter sipped his water and wiped the moisture from his hands on the napkin in his lap. "That was good to hear. He said he'll check in with me again toward the end of the semester."

"Wonderful!" Kenya fingered the rim of her glass. "So far, they truly like what they see. I would just be careful about how you interact with your students on campus. Otherwise, I'd say things are looking good for you."

"Really." Hunter raised his brow.

Kenya smiled. "Did you know Professor Silverstein is being honored by some organization in a few weeks?"

Kenya pushed the food around on her plate. "The department is holding a reception for him. You should come. It would be a good opportunity for you to network. In addition to the department head, a few board members will be in attendance."

"Let me check my calendar. If I don't have any prior commitments, I'll be there."

"Good."

Hunter's appetite wasn't as robust as when he first arrived. He waved the waiter over. "I'd like to take this to go."

The young man nodded politely and took his plate.

"You didn't finish," Kenya said.

"I'll eat the rest later. I need to head out."

"Oh…okay." Kenya looked disappointed. She led the conversation further with trivial small talk until the waiter returned with Hunter's doggie bag and the bill.

Hunter pulled out his credit card and handed it to the waiter.

"Wait!" Kenya twisted to retrieve her wallet.

Hunter held up his hand. "That won't be necessary."

"Oh, thanks, Hunter. You didn't have to do that."

"It was my pleasure." The smile that spread across Kenya's lips made Hunter think he should have chosen different words.

Kenya and Hunter said their goodbyes and he headed for the train back to Brooklyn. The moment he ascended the steps at his stop, he called Chey. No answer. He wondered who the student was whom Chey apparently connected with. That might have been the reason she'd acted so distant earlier. The jealous pang hadn't surprised him. He didn't bother denying this affection for Chey. Technically, Hunter couldn't seriously date her without jeopardizing the opportunities in front of him, but he hadn't thought about the possibility of her dating someone else. Suddenly, he felt possessive. Pulling out his phone, he dialed Chey again. *Damn.* Still no answer. He shoved the phone back in his pocket. Maybe her strange behavior wasn't about a fellow student at all. At least he hoped it wasn't. Maybe something was wrong and she wasn't able to talk about it at school. Besides, had she picked up the phone, he couldn't promise that he wouldn't have asked her about the fellow classmate Kenya spoke of, despite knowing it wasn't his place.

Hunter's cell phone rang. He couldn't get it out of his pocket quick enough. His enthusiasm deflated when he saw that it was his brother calling.

"What's up, little bro? Are you in town?" Hunter was happy to hear from his youngest brother. It had been at least a week since their last conversation. They communicated frequently on the brothers' instant-messaging group chat, but it was always nice to hear his voice.

"I'll be there in a couple of weeks. I wanted to get on your calendar now. I know how busy you can be. Plus Blake said you had a new honey."

"Ha!" Hunter chose not to address the "new honey" comment. "It doesn't matter. I can always make time for my bigheaded little brother."

"Yeah. Whatever." Drew chuckled. "I'm going to stay at Mom and Dad's."

"Really. No lucky woman has the good fortune to have you warm her bed during your visit?"

"I didn't say all of that, now. I'll just be at Mom and Dad's for the weekend."

"Ha! Now, that's the Drew I know! Have I met this one?"

"I doubt it."

"Will I meet her?"

"Probably not!"

"Ha! Cool. I look forward to meeting the one that claims your heart." Hunter chuckled at Drew's rambunctious laugh. "Have you spoken to Blake yet?"

"I started in age order. He's my next call."

"Okay. We'll catch up when I get there." Hunter turned onto his block.

"All right. See you soon, big bro."

"Be safe."

Hunter's mind turned back to Chey as he ended the call and trotted up the few steps to his brownstone. He had shared Chey's interest in working for Estelle London with Blake, who knew a woman who worked there. They had a competitive apprenticeship opportunity for recent grads that Chey would be excited to hear about. That was what he'd wanted to tell her earlier. Also, a client had given him a pair of tickets to the Broadway show *The Phantom of the Opera* for this weekend. All day Hunter had anticipated Chey's excitement when he shared the news with her.

Hunter showered, threw on a fresh pair of boxers and flopped on his bed with his remote in hand. Deciding to give it one last try, he dialed Chey's number. This time it went straight to voice mail. The message he left detailed all that she needed to do to apply for the apprenticeship program with Estelle London before sharing the news about the tickets to the show.

Hunter sat with his back against the plush leather headboard, flipping through the channels. A while later, his phone dinged, indicating that he'd received an email. Chey responded to his voice message with a cordial email thanking him for the information about the opportunity at Estelle London and politely declining his offer of the show tickets. Hunter was puzzled. He went to bed wondering what he had done to warrant this uncharacteristic behavior from Chey. Then he thought about Kenya's not-so-subtle warning about being careful with his interactions with students. Maybe it was best that he left things between Chey and him the way they were. He didn't like that idea but what other choice did he have?

Chapter 24

Inadvertently, Chey had thought keeping her distance from Hunter would get easier. Instead, she missed him immensely—his smile, the way he thoughtfully considered her and his fun nature. Spring had made an appearance and her feelings for Hunter hadn't diminished at all. Seeing him twice a week was torturous. Kenya added to this torture by parading her chumminess with Hunter in front of Chey. She cringed inwardly every time she saw her touch his arm as they spoke or throw her head back and laugh as if his words tickled every one of her fancies. She never failed to glance Chey's way to make sure she was taking it all in.

Chey found herself wondering if Hunter missed her, too. Her insides were filled with nervous energy as she fretted over the midsemester meeting that was scheduled after today's class. This would be the first time in weeks that she and Hunter would share the same space—privately. These advisory meetings, which he'd already held with half the class, were designed to assess where the students were in respect to where they needed to be by the end of the semester.

The nervous energy had reached a nauseating high by the time class was over. Hunter had one student to see before meeting with her, which gave her an additional half hour to agonize. Her time had come and the trek to Hunter's office felt like a trudge down the green mile. It was no surprise that Kenya stood leaning against her doorway with her arms folded across her chest and her eyes glued to Chey.

Chey had already endured her mid-semester meeting with Kenya, who'd not-so-subtly reminded her to keep her distance when it came to Hunter.

When Chey reached Hunter's door, she looked back and Kenya was still watching her. Turning, she rolled her eyes as she knocked. Out walked a fellow classmate. Chey stepped aside to let him pass and Hunter invited her in.

The air in his office seemed so much thicker than the last time she was in there.

"Ms. Rodgers." He smiled and nodded cordially, motioning for her to take a seat before taking one himself.

"So," Hunter began.

"So," Chey repeated, wringing her hands.

Hunter watched her for a moment and cleared his throat. He opened an agenda and flipped to a page with her name at the top.

"You're on track for ending the semester with an A. You did very well on the midterm." Chey watched Hunter's eyes as they scanned the paper. "What are your plans from here, Ms. Rodgers?"

Chey wanted to tell him to stop addressing her as Ms. Rodgers. It sounded too impersonal.

"To continue on this path. I'd like to end the semester with a four-point-oh across the board."

"Really! How's that looking for you?"

"Good so far." Chey returned her attention to her fingers as she picked her nails.

Hunters gaze was penetrating. When Chey looked up, she focused on the shelf of books behind him so she wouldn't get lost in his probing dark eyes.

"There's not much more to review regarding your work. Do you have any questions for me?"

Do you miss me? Of course, that would be deemed inappropriate. *Do you like Kenya?* Chey assumed that wouldn't fly either. She'd never been the jealous type and didn't enjoy feeling that way now. "I don't think so."

Hunter stood, walked toward her. Chey's breath caught. Why was he getting so close? He continued past Chey and stood silently by the door for a moment. After another beat, he opened the door slightly and closed it again. Chey almost expected Kenya to fall in when he did that.

Hunter sat back in his chair and after another brief moment went by, he leaned forward.

"So how is everything else? Are you still exploring the Big Apple?"

"Honestly, not as much." *Especially without my personal tour guide.*

"That's too bad. Did you ever pursue that program with Estelle London?"

"Oh! Yeah. Thanks again for that information. I submitted my application, but I haven't heard anything back."

"When do you anticipate hearing from them?"

"Hopefully, before the end of the semester. If not, I'll be headed back to Virginia."

"You're going back home?" Hunter sat erect. His brows knitted.

"Yes. I really only came for school and hoped to land a job with one of the cosmetic companies by the time school ended. So far that hasn't happened and New York is quite an expensive city. At least at home, I have somewhat of a clientele. I'll continue to work on my line and maybe start my own company. I just thought it would be ideal to work with one of the industry giants for a while. That way I could learn the other aspects of the business."

"Hmm. I hope something comes through."

"Me, too." Neither of them spoke for a while. Chey tried to avoid staring at the way his muscular arms strained against his dress shirt. Hunter, on the other hand, hadn't bothered hiding his hunger and lapped her up with his sparkling brown orbs. Chey would have considered this kind of study from any other man inappropriate. It was not only welcome but a pleasing confirmation that it was possible that he'd missed her, too.

"What about you? How are things going? Will you be coming back as a permanent professor next semester?"

"Things are looking good, but I don't want to speak too soon. I won't know for sure until my review in May."

"How's the legal business treating you?"

"All is well."

"That's good to hear." Chey cast her eyes toward her lap.

Weighted silence filled the space once again with things desired but left unsaid.

"If there's nothing else, I guess I'll be going." She dared to meet his eyes once again.

"Yeah. I think we're good." Hunter licked his lips, then sighed. "Oh. Have you taken in a Broadway show yet?"

"Unfortunately, no! Also, thanks again for offering me your tickets for *Phantom of the Opera*. I wish I could have taken you up on that."

Chey wondered if he had taken anyone else to see it after she declined. "Did you see it?"

"No."

Chey was relieved. Maybe that was something they

could do together before she headed back home. It would be her treat. She sighed at the thought of leaving Hunter behind in New York, but without a decent full-time job, she'd have to return to Virginia, and so far she hadn't received any callbacks from the many companies she'd applied to. Her savings would eventually run out and she wouldn't be able to afford New York living.

"Well." Hunter glanced at his watch and then stood. Chey took that as a sign that their meeting was over."

Chey stood, too, and faced the door, turning her back to Hunter. She felt his hand on her arm and it sent a sensual volt through her. Slowly, she turned to meet Hunter face-to-face.

"I miss…" Hunter paused. Chey held her breath. She longed to hear him say he missed her. "…talking to you."

Chey was offended. He missed talking to her, but apparently, he hadn't missed *her* in the same way that she'd been missing him. Obviously, the distance affected them differently.

"Yeah. Take care, Professor." She couldn't help the sting that showed up in her words.

Hunter's door swung open. That was when Chey noticed that his hand was still on her arm. He released her abruptly, but not before Kenya saw it. Her eyes followed Hunter's hand from Chey's arm back to his side.

"Oh, sorry! I thought you were done. I was wondering if we were going to grab a bite before heading home."

Liar! Kenya's audacity irked Chey. She held her tongue but kept her eyes pinned on Kenya. "We're done." She turned back toward Hunter. "Thanks, Professor. I'll see you in class next week. Have a great weekend."

Striding around Kenya, Chey speed-walked down the hall and continued her quick pace until she reached her train station. The jealousy stung. By the time she made it home, she was wound tight. Taking her steps two at a time, she reached her floor in seconds. Inside her apartment, she dropped her bag on the couch and paced back and forth. Somehow strong feelings for Hunter had rooted themselves deep within her system. Now it seemed as though there was even less of a chance they'd end up together, even after the semester was done. She'd have to work on forgetting about him—somehow.

Chapter 25

Chey was moving back to Virginia. That singular thought had robbed Hunter of precious sleep. He couldn't let that happen. Yes. He liked her—a lot. So much that he wasn't willing to see her go. Seeing her and not being able to touch her was hard enough, but he didn't want to cause her any more trouble with Kenya. He noticed the way Kenya treated Chey and only hoped the jealousy wouldn't affect her grades. She was a diligent student who worked hard. He couldn't wait until the semester ended so that he could pursue her without restraint, but she was moving.

Hunter marched into Blake's office. He had an idea.

"Blake!"

Blake's head snapped up. "What's up, bro?"

"Your friend who works for Estelle London—are you able to get in touch with her?"

"Sure, why?"

"I need your help with something." Hunter told Blake what he needed him to do and then went back to his office.

Hunter looked up Chey's parents' shop in Virginia, called them up and placed an order and then sat back hoping this would work. Hopefully, Chey would appreciate what he was trying to do for her, but he could also see how she might perceive his actions as meddling. If she got angry with him for trying to help her out, then he'd have to deal with it. As long as she was able to stay in New York after graduation, it would all be worth it. He'd keep this to himself until he saw how it all panned out.

Hunter's cell phone rang, breaking into his thoughts. It was Kenya.

"Hello."

"Hey there," she crooned. "We're still on for tonight, right?"

We? What was she talking about? Had he offered to take her out? Since Chey hadn't been around, he had spent much more time with Kenya. Despite her insistent flirtation, they had actually become closer—as friends. She was fun to be around, but he hoped that she wasn't getting the wrong idea. It wouldn't be the first time a woman took his friendliness for something entirely different. He'd have to work on managing Kenya's expectations carefully. Her input was instrumental in helping him get the position. "What are we supposed to be on for?"

"The reception in honor of Professor Silverstein's awards," she said as if she couldn't believe he'd forgotten.

Hunter released the breath he'd been holding. "Oh, that!"

"You're still coming, right?"

"Yes."

"I was thinking we could go together. What time would you like to meet?"

"I'm coming straight from work, so how about I just meet you there?"

"Oh…okay."

Hunter sensed that she didn't like his answer. "What time does it start?" he asked.

"Six thirty."

"Okay. See you then."

Hunter finished his day and prepared his mind for dealing with Kenya at the reception. She was insistent and a tad sneaky with a bit of an underhanded side that was most evident in her dealings with Chey. Hunter did recall Eric mentioning her being strong willed when she wanted something. Hunter assumed that could be both good and bad.

As the work day ended, Hunter told Blake about the reception and promised to catch up with him later that night. Drew was in town and they were going to meet up for drinks. Hunter planned to show his face at the reception, shake a few hands and make an inconspicuous exit.

When Hunter arrived at the university, Kenya met him at the entrance to the building. Snaking her arm around his, she led him to the conference room where the reception was being held. The large wood table that normally commanded the center of the room had been placed against the back wall and was covered with refreshments, an ice bucket and several bottles of wine.

Kenya paraded him around the room, introducing him to those he hadn't met. He finally managed to break free of her grasp, but not from her line of sight.

"Professor Silverstein." Hunter approached the honoree and shook his hand.

"Hunter! Please call me Ed," he said with a broad smile.

"Ed." Hunter smiled back. "I just want to congratulate you on being honored. I took the liberty of looking into it and I think the research you've done on the changes in the modern workplace is impressive and right on target."

"Thanks, Hunter." Ed patted Hunter's arm. "Much appreciated."

"I need to get a copy of your recent book. I'm sure I

can find some information in there that I could apply to my own business."

"You run your own practice, right?"

"Yes, along with my brother Blake. My father started the practice years ago before becoming a judge and passing it on to us."

"Impressive! And from what I understand, you're one fine lawyer, so what brings you here to Dunford?"

"Our family has always been service oriented. Giving back is a priority. Like many, I donate to charities, but for me, being a professor is one of the most profound ways to be of service, and since Dunford is my alma mater, I don't believe there's a better way for me to offer my services than to help students here get ready for the real world. I've always valued the lessons I learned from my professors."

Martin Powell, the department head, and another professor approached Hunter and Ed as they spoke.

"I was just congratulating Ed on his many accomplishments," Hunter humbly stated.

"Yes," Martin said with a proud smile and approving nod in Ed's direction. "The department is lucky to have him." Martin turned to Hunter. "And from what I understand, we're pretty lucky to have you, too. I've been hearing good things."

Hunter's flashed his most winning smile. "Thanks, Martin. I was just telling Ed that this is something that I've wanted to do for a long time. Teaching for me is my way of giving back to the community."

"I hear you're firm but fair and the students seem to really like your teaching style."

"Ha! From what I understand, they like more than his teaching style. This dapper chap has some of the female students smitten." Hunter hadn't seen Kenya sidle up to the group.

On the outside, Hunter smiled and dismissed her comment with a simple wave, but under the surface, he began to boil.

"Yeah, well, that happens! I got a lot more of that when I had more hair." Martin ran his hand over his thinning gray hairline and roared. They all laughed. Martin's comment had taken the pressure off him.

Hunter flashed Kenya a scolding expression covered by a smile that could have been misconstrued as friendly by onlookers. It was obvious that she'd had a little too much wine. She winked back. Hunter decided he'd take that inconspicuous exit sooner than planned.

"I haven't exactly had that problem," Ed said, slapping his round belly. All of them continued to laugh. "I'm all brains! Beauty, well, it depends on who's looking. My wife is stuck with me now."

Hunter laughed along with his colleagues until Kenya opened up her mouth again. "Well, they get a real charge out of Hunter here." Hunter modestly stretched his eyes at Kenya, hoping she'd catch the hint and stop talking. "You should have seen it. His first day, students were gathered outside his class snickering like preteens. I even had a chat with one in particular." Hunter's smile had all but faded. The remnant was purely for the benefit of Ed and Martin. Kenya looked directly at Hunter and continued, "Yeah, I had to let her know she needed to stand down." Kenya threw her head back and laughed.

Hunter gauged his colleagues' expressions. Martin's and Ed's smiles were gone, as well. Hunter couldn't believe that Kenya had said those things in front of them. The angry fire that she had sparked with her earlier actions now burned fiercely. A consummate professional with an expert poker face—thanks to his legal training—Hunter took her comment in stride, chuckled and slightly turned his back to Kenya. The message was clear. She had all but said Chey's name.

"The last thing that concerns me is a schoolgirl's crush. I'm a Barrington. We are men of character and integrity. I'm here for a much greater purpose and that's my focus."

"I hear you." Martin patted Hunter's back. "You're indeed a professional, Hunter." Martin turned to each of the others with a polite nod. "Now if you'll excuse us—" he directed his next comment to Hunter "—I'd like to chat with you for a quick moment."

Adrenaline coursed through Hunter's veins with fervor. "Sure." He hoped his nervousness didn't show. Without looking back at Kenya, he knew that she was watching.

Contrary to what Hunter expected, Martin simply wanted to ask a few questions about how he thought the experience was going. He also told Hunter that he wanted to get a date scheduled for his review soon and then asked how he felt about the possibility of being on the board. Hunter acted genuinely surprised when Martin mentioned the board appointment. He'd complied with Kenya's request for nondisclosure. Unfortunately, he couldn't say the same for her.

Someone tapped a glass, capturing the attention of Martin, Hunter and everyone else in the room. Another colleague announced that it was time for a toast. People cheered and took turns offering congratulations and kind words to Ed. Hunter said his piece, and as they continued to go around the room, he made his exit.

Halfway down the street, his phone rang. Kenya was looking for him. Hunter sent the call to voice mail and then tapped out a text letting his brothers know he was on his way. He really needed a drink.

Chapter 26

Deanna stepped into Chey's apartment and paused. "This is…" she looked around while fishing for the right word "…cozy!"

"Stop your lying!" Chey laughed. She grabbed Deanna's bag and walked past her. "It's downright tiny, but it was all I could afford without a roommate."

Deanna looked at her and cracked up laughing. "Okay. It's minuscule. In Virginia, this entire apartment would fit in our bathroom. Ha!"

"Now you're exaggerating—a little." She chuckled all six steps into her bedroom and rolled Deanna's suitcase into a corner. "Now go shower," she ordered Deanna as she headed back to the living room. "So you can wash off that bus funk and get cute. We're hanging out tonight."

"Whoo," Deanna squealed. "I can't wait." She stood in the center of the room with her hands on her hips, looking around. "I'm in my sister's apartment in New York City." Deanna pulled Chey into a tight embrace. "You're really doing this. I'm so proud of you."

Chey heard a sniffle. Snapping her head back, she looked into Deanna's glistening eyes. "Are you crying?"

"Who, me?" Deanna quickly let her go, turned her back and wiped her tears. "Of course not."

Chey shook her head. "Come here." She hugged her sister again. "I can't believe you. You're such a crybaby," Chey teased. Deanna laughed through her tears. "Now get your butt in the shower," Chey ordered and sealed her directive with a playful shove.

"Momma and Daddy are so proud of you. They've told everyone about you living in the big city." Deanna spoke as she shuffled through her bag for something to wear. "The people at church think you're big-time now. You know what small-town folk think of the big city. To them, moving to New York is like becoming a movie star."

"I know." Chey chuckled. "So Mom is proud, huh? I'd never think so with the grief Mom gives me about being here alone." Deanna's statement was bittersweet for Chey. She was happy to make her family proud, but what would they say when she was on their doorstep with nothing more than a degree in her hand? What would Todd say? She recalled his words. *When this silly plan of yours fails, you'll be back.* She'd never live it down if he turned out to be right. She'd come to New York to make it big. Casting those thoughts aside, Chey went into the bedroom to help Deanna pick an outfit.

"Oh, this is nice!" Chey held up a long black shirt with a lace back. "Did you bring leggings?"

"Yep." Deanna dug in the bag and pulled out a black pair.

Chey put the shirt down and ran to her closet. "I have the perfect boots for you to wear with them."

Deanna's eyes stretched at the sight of the tall riding boots Chey held up. "Cute!"

"Now hurry up. I need to get dressed, too," Chey commanded.

A while later both were dressed for a night out, Deanna in the outfit her sister had picked and Chey in a flowing black top, skinny jeans and high-heeled booties.

They shared the small bathroom mirror. Chey was fixing her hair while Deanna applied foundation.

"Let me make up your face?" Deanna twisted her lips as she rubbed blush into her cheeks. Chey just frowned.

"Eyeliner and gloss are enough for me."

"Come on. You have such a pretty face. You'll look amazing."

"Whatever." Chey shrugged and let Deanna do as she pleased. When she was done, Chey looked in the mirror and was awed by her reflection. She had to admit, the makeup did enhance her features. Her brown eyes popped. "Wow."

"See! I told you."

"Whatever!" Chey headed to the bedroom and flipped through her closet in search of a light scarf to go with her leather jacket.

Deanna came in behind her and flopped on the bed. There was a crack and then a loud bang. The edge of the bed sunk and Deanna fell right into the large cavity it created.

"Ah!" Deanna screamed.

Chey's hands flew to her mouth. "Oh my goodness! How did that happen?"

"I don't know. Just get me out."

Chey ran to Deanna and pulled her up. "My bed!" she whined.

"We've got to fix this. How are we going to sleep tonight?" Deanna pulled the mattress up to reveal several broken wood slats. "Chey, it was just a matter of time before this broke. What have you been doing in here?" Deanna eyed her suspiciously.

Chey clucked her tongue. "Move, silly." She surveyed the damage. "I can't fix this."

"Call the super."

"I can only call him if something is wrong with the apartment, like plumbing or the heat. This bed is my problem." Chey let the mattress slip from her hand. "Besides, the super creeps me out. Ugh! He has such a sleazy demeanor and looks at me like he wants to rip my clothes off. I don't want him touching my bed."

"You need to call someone. Who can help us out with this?"

Chey thought about Hunter but dismissed the idea as quickly as it came. Besides, when she saw him at school, she hadn't spoken to him.

"What about the professor?"

"I can't call him."

"Why not? He wouldn't help you?"

"Of course he would, but I haven't spoken to him in a while."

"Do you know of any other guy that could help out? We can't do this by ourselves." Deanna shook her head.

"Not really." Chey hadn't bothered becoming friendly with many people, especially men.

"Then call him! We can't leave the bed like this. That couch—" Deanna pointed toward the living room "—isn't big enough for the two of us."

Reluctantly, Chey dialed Hunter's number. Fortunately, he picked up right away. She apologized for bothering him and explained her plight. Hunter said he was already in Manhattan and would be right there.

"Told you!" Deanna said.

"Hush it!" Chey said and laughed. Since they were kids, they'd loved to playfully rub things in each other's faces.

A while later Hunter, along with two replicas who varied in shades of brown showed up at her door. Deanna discreetly stretched her eyes at Chey and mouthed, *Oh my God!* They were equally tall, chocolatey and gorgeous. Hunter and Blake were dressed smartly in blue and gray suits, respectively. Drew, the apparent rebel, sported jeans, boots and a black-and-green motorcycle jacket.

"Hi, Hunter. Thanks so much for coming by on such short notice." To Chey's surprise, Hunter leaned over, embraced her and gave her a friendly kiss on the cheek. She wanted to melt.

"This is my sister, Deanna."

Deanna held her hand out. "Nice to meet you, Hunter."

"These are my brothers, Blake and Drew."

"Blake." Chey nodded. "Drew." She nodded again. "I'm Chey." They all shook hands.

"Take me to the problem," Hunter said.

They followed Chey and Deanna into the room. Chey was glad that she had cleaned up thoroughly in preparation for Deanna's visit. Together the brothers assessed the problem, lifting the mattress and examining the broken wood underneath.

"Whoa, girl! What have you been doing in here?" Drew laughed. Deanna's eyes widened as she hid a laugh behind her shocked expression. Chey froze as embarrassment burned her cheeks.

"I wasn't…"

"Drew! Cut it out," Hunter said, chuckling. "I'm supposed to ask that." His sexy eyes landed on Chey and hers stretched wider.

"Don't pay them any mind." That was Blake.

The weight of shame lifted off Chey when everyone in the room burst out laughing. She joined in. When the laughter subsided, the men talked about what was needed to fix her bed. Hunter checked his phone to find out which hardware stores were still open. The men left and returned within the hour with several two-by-fours and tools.

Chey pulled out a few chilled bottles of water and got out of their way as they began clearing broken wood. Something radiated inside her when Hunter removed his suit jacket and shirt, revealing a taut chest and muscular build through his undershirt. Blake and Drew had done the same, but they didn't have an effect on Chey. Drew openly flirted with Deanna and she giggled as if she were back in middle school.

"Chey!" Hunter called her over. "We're going to need some music while we work. This looks like it may take a while."

"Oh! Sure. Let me put something on." Chey set her music app to an R & B station.

"And some food, too! Order some pizza—I'm paying!" Drew instructed.

Chey laughed as she picked up the phone and called her favorite pizza shop. It felt good having Hunter in her home. She watched his muscles move as he worked. A few times he caught her ogling him and smiled. They labored diligently until a really good song would come on and one of the brothers would start hooting and dancing, rendering each of them unproductive until the song changed. Chey and Deanna cracked up watching them interact or fuss about who wasn't holding what right. They took a break when the pizza came, but the antics continued right through the meal.

The conversation moved to any embarrassing story they could tell about Hunter from back in the day. The one about Hunter being hit in the head with a football while his teenage crush watched had everyone doubled over. Drew acted out the entire story. Chey could hardly catch her breath.

Hunter tossed his shirt at his brother and told them of

the time when Drew was in grade school and a pretty little girl down the block kissed him. Drew had gotten so excited he'd wet his pants.

"Dude, I was five!" Drew tried to defend himself.

When the pizza was done, the brothers resumed working, and within the hour, Chey's bed was fixed.

Chey locked eyes with Hunter as they said their goodbyes.

"Thanks again. I didn't want to bother you, but I didn't know who else to call."

"It's not a problem at all. Call me anytime."

An awkward silence ensued and was broken when Drew cleared his throat. "Just go ahead and kiss her, man. You know you want to," he teased. "I'm just joking. It was nice meeting you, Chey." He looked Deanna up and down and licked his lips. "You, too, Ms. Deanna."

Deanna blushed and shook her head. "Bye, Drew!" They carried on like old friends.

"We're going for a few drinks. You ladies should join us," Blake added. Hunter and Chey looked at each other.

"Uh…thanks, but I'm really tired," Chey said, ignoring the sideways glare Deanna tossed in her direction. The knowing look Hunter cast her way confirmed that he understood. As much as she wanted to stay in Hunter's presence, she knew it wasn't a good idea. Kenya's warning came to mind. "You gentlemen have fun."

Hunter was the last to leave. He gave her another friendly hug and kiss on the cheek. This one was much closer to her lips. Chey closed the door slowly and leaned against it. When she looked up, Deanna was in her face.

"What the heck was that?" Deanna asked.

Chey would explain in the morning. Right now she needed to remember how to breathe.

Chapter 27

Spring break had been anything but a break for Hunter. Seeing Chey at her apartment had brought feelings to the surface that he'd thought he had buried. One of his pro bono clients had cracked under the pressure of a cross-examination. He'd jumped over the witness stand and choked the attorney who was badgering him. His face had been plastered on the front page of every newspaper and television screen in the metropolitan area. The incident weakened any progress they had made, forcing him to work around the clock and add damage control to his repertoire of skills.

Hunter's only reprieve was the fact that he didn't have to deal with Kenya. He was still quite upset after she showed out at Ed's reception. He wanted to ask about the comments she'd made pertaining to Chey. Was it true that Kenya had told her to "stand down"?

Kenya had been calling him all week, but he wanted to speak with her face-to-face.

Just as he expected, Kenya was standing by his door when he arrived for class.

"Hey, Hunter." Her smile was weak and full of guilt.

"Hello, Kenya." He continued past her.

"Can we talk after class?"

"Sure. See you then."

Hunter went straight into the room and addressed his class. Gone was the usual enthusiasm that made him such an engaging professor.

"Let's get right to the..." His eyes landed on Chey. He remembered how beautiful she'd looked the night he went to her house to fix her bed. She'd had on makeup then and looked like a movie star. She was still beautiful now. He remembered that he was addressing his class "...presentations that you were assigned over the break." He continued pulling away from her magnetism. There was so much he wanted to say to her. She had returned to behaving like a cordial stranger. "Would someone like to volunteer or should I call names by alpha order?"

"I'll go." One of his most confident and argumentative students stood. Hunter thought he'd make a better attorney than businessman.

In the assignment, students had to examine contracts for possible loopholes and present a scenario that would bring the issue to light and offer a possible resolution. Hunter trained them to look at contracts not for what they said but for what they often left unsaid that could be problematic for a business owner.

There was enough time for half the class to present. After the presentations, Hunter walked around the room distributing handouts outlining the requirements for their final projects. He couldn't believe they were almost at the end of the semester. Chey could be leaving for Virginia soon.

"You may select one of the options listed on this paper. For example, you can choose intellectual property, contracts, et cetera. Read this carefully. Points will be added or removed depending on how well you adhered to the instructions. I'm completely confident that if you apply yourselves, you'll all do well. On Thursday, we will continue with the presentations. In the meantime, have a great night."

In the next instant, the only sounds you could hear were footsteps and chairs scraping the floor as students departed the class.

Hunter hung back until the last student had left. He watched Chey purposely avoid him as she walked out. Grabbing his briefcase, he headed for his tête-à-tête with Kenya. She was waiting outside her office. Hunter walked past her and straight into his office. He was going to have this conversation on his turf.

Closing the door behind her, she started right away. "I want to apologize." She sat slowly. Hunter remained standing. "I was out of line at the reception that night. I don't know what got into me." She stopped talking. Hunter remained tight-lipped. He wanted to hear what she had to say before he started. "It will never happen again."

"I'm sure it won't." Kenya hung her head sideways. She looked confused. "Can I ask you a question?"

"Sure, Hunter. Ask me anything."

"Have you ever had a conversation with Chey Rodgers concerning me?"

Kenya's mouth opened and closed a few times before words stumbled past her lips. "I was just looking out for you. I didn't want anyone to see how cozy you two were and think there was something going on. I know how bad you wanted this to work. Someone may have said something. I didn't want…" she babbled.

Hunter shook his head and gnawed the inside of his bottom lip. He had a feeling that Kenya had done more meddling than he knew about. Keeping his anger at bay was a struggle. "What did you say to her?" Hunter cut off her rambling.

"Uh…nothing bad. I…I just…"

"What did you say to her, Kenya?" His harsh tone startled her, and for a moment, she stared at him.

She looked down. "I told her to stay away from you."

Hunter slammed his palm against the desk. "Are you serious?" He rubbed his hand down his face. This explained the abrupt shift in her attitude toward him. No wonder she would never call him back. He'd left dozens of messages before he finally stopped calling altogether.

"It was for your own good."

"Mine or yours?"

Kenya's mouth opened again, but nothing came out.

Hunter paced the small space, contemplating his next words. "I was surprised at your lack of professionalism at the reception." He paused to make sure he had her full attention. He did. "While I appreciate any assistance you offered in helping me acquire this adjunct professor opportunity, rest assured that it was my hard work, credentials and merit that ultimately secured the position and it will be those same things that help me keep it. I've done a damn good job and have given my all. I certainly don't appreciate my integrity being undermined by underhanded tactics. At one point, I enjoyed getting to know you. Now I know more than I ever cared to. At this point, it's best that we keep our interactions strictly professional. If this opportunity is meant for me, then I will get it. If not…well, there are other universities." Hunter finally sat down with his hand at his chin. "Have a good night, Professor Davis."

"Hunter." Kenya stood abruptly. "It doesn't have to be like this. We may be working together. We should at least be friends."

"I have a hard time being friends with people that I can't trust."

Kenya gasped. For a second, Hunter thought she was about to cry. He took out his cell phone and started scrolling through emails. He refused to be manipulated by her any further. Kenya remained still for a few moments before slowly turning to leave.

Hunter stayed in his office until she'd left. He didn't want to risk running into her on the way out. Instead, he spent that time talking to his brothers, filling them in on the latest details.

"That's crazy. You need to watch her, bro," Drew said.

"I can't expend my energy that way. I don't like drama."

"You did the right thing," Blake affirmed. "I can't believe she tried to sabotage your relationship with Chey."

"I still need to be careful."

"Right," Blake added. "You have to make it through your review or at least past her graduation."

"Unfortunately, she might move back to Virginia after graduation."

"Why?" both brothers asked.

"If one of those jobs doesn't manifest, she won't be able to afford to stay."

"There's always your house!" Drew teased. As much as Hunter liked the idea, Chey would never agree to that. "What's stopping you from still seeing her? Virginia is a short plane ride away," Drew said.

"Long-distance relationships are not for me."

"Anything will work with the right woman."

"Drew!" Blake admonished. "What do you know about the right woman?" All of them laughed. "Seriously, Hunter," Blake continued. "It sounds like you really care about her."

"I do."

"Then you have a lot to think about, but you can't actually make a move until she graduates."

"I know, and then it might be too late." Hunter left his office and talked to his brothers until he reached the train station. I'll figure something out," he said before saying goodbye and ending the call.

Chey occupied his mind as he rode the subway back to Brooklyn. Maybe what Kenya had done was best. The lines of friendship he'd hoped to develop with Chey had quickly become marred by his yearning for her. He remembered the few times they'd kissed, which had left them wanting so much more. Who knew what would have happened had they not put some distance between them? His desire for Chey could have blinded his judgment and he might have risked everything that he'd worked for. The only thing left to do now was wait.

When Hunter rose from the subway, his phone dinged several times with alerts from social media posts, texts and emails. He checked his email and sighed at the memo from Martin about wanting to speak with him. "What is it now?" he wondered aloud. Had Kenya spoken to him after their discussion?

Chapter 28

Chey tried her best to maintain some excitement in her voice as she reminisced with her sister and mother about Deanna's recent trip to New York.

"Mom, you should have seen Chey showing me around as if she'd lived in the city all her life. I had such a great time."

"Honey, I'd love to do a little sightseeing when your dad and I come up for your graduation. Your aunt Opal is going to mind the shop while we're gone. I have to admit, now that Deanna's told me all about her stay, I feel a little better about you being there—just a little." They all laughed.

"Chey, you have to take Mom to the fashion district. She's gonna love that. Oh! That museum that you took me to that looks like a work of art itself," Deanna gasped. "I've never seen a building like that before in my entire life. What's it's called, again? The Googleheim."

That elicited a laugh from Chey. "No, silly. It's the Guggenheim. Say it with me. Gug-gen-heim!"

Deanna and her mother carried the conversation with little input from Chey. She listened, chiming in here and there, until Deanna noticed that she hadn't said much.

"Chey. What's wrong?"

"Huh?" Chey had been sitting on the couch leaning against the arm. Now she sat up. "Why do you ask that?"

"You just don't sound like your usual self. Is everything okay with school?"

"Oh. Sure. I'm just a little tired. Working on these final projects has definitely affected my sleep."

"Oh. Okay." Deanna didn't sound convinced.

"Well, that will all be over within another week. I can't wait to see you walk across that stage. Oh! I'm so proud of you, baby."

"Thanks, Mom. I need to get back to my assignments. I'll chat with you guys later. Don't forget to let me know when your bus gets in so I can be there to meet you all."

"I hope you canceled that hotel reservation. I told you to save your money! Dad and I can sleep at your place."

"No! I insist. I want you and Dad to have a great New York experience." Chey was adamant. "It's just one night and it's already paid for. I booked it through one of the discount travel sites."

"Mom! Didn't I tell you the girl lives in a boot box? It's a little bigger than a shoe box. Where are you, Dad and I supposed to sleep?" Deanna hooted.

"Deanna!" their mother chided. "That's not nice."

"Oh, but it's true, Mom!" Chey added. "Now hush it, Deanna!" The girls laughed. "I gotta go, so I'll chat with you later. Love you."

"Love you, too, sweetheart." Patricia kissed her through the phone.

"Later, sis."

After ending the call, Chey tossed the phone to the other end of the couch and sighed. She thought about starting to pack but decided to wait. Her parents would want to see her apartment and she didn't want to have to explain the boxes. She was hopeful that either the apprenticeship opportunity or one of the other jobs she had applied for would come through at the last minute and she wouldn't have to go back home. If not, then she would pack up after graduation and let her landlord know that she would be gone by the end of May. Initially, she'd intended to live out her one-year lease, which would end in October, but without another job, that wouldn't be possible.

Chey's phone rang and she reached for it begrudgingly. Right now she wasn't in the mood to talk, but she looked to see who was calling anyway. When she saw Hunter's name, she answered immediately.

"Hello."

"Hey."

"Hunter. It's nice to hear from you." She meant it. The last time they had a real conversation was when he and his brothers came to fix her bed.

"It's good to hear from you, too. How's the final project coming along?"

"Actually, it's coming along well and it's so interesting. I chose to do my study on Estelle London and I've found out so much about the company in my research, but that's all I will say."

"Ha! I'll see it when you hand your project in."

"Exactly."

"I wanted to say one thing." Hunter's tone became serious, putting Chey on alert.

"Sure."

"I know that Kenya said something to you about staying away from me." Chey's eyes widened as she listened more intently. "I didn't ask her to do that and I just want to apologize for her behavior and mine."

"Yours?"

"Yes. I know she didn't make this semester easy for you, but I'm also apologizing because I should have been more careful. I knew trying to be 'friends' with you was risky since, honestly, I wanted more." Chey's hand flew to her mouth. "And still do." Chey balked. "But it wasn't smart to jeopardize your or my position, so I'm sorry. I hope that once you graduate, maybe we can start fresh."

"That would be nice." What should have made Chey excited, actually made her feel dejected. She couldn't bring herself to tell him she probably wouldn't be around long enough for a fresh start.

"Is your family coming up for your graduation?"

"Of course, but they're only staying one night. I'm going to take them sightseeing the day before and they have to head back home after graduation.

"Would it be okay if I took you to dinner after graduation to celebrate?"

"Oh! You don't have to do that, Hunter, but it would be nice."

"Ha! I think you're going to enjoy it."

"So are you asking me out on a date? Because when we went out before, it wasn't a date."

"Oh! You'll no longer be off-limits. This will be a date for sure. I want a kiss at the end of the night and all."

Chey's laugh generated from her core. "Okay, Professor Barrington!

"As for now, Ms. Rodgers, get to work on that final project. It better be worthy of an A!"

"Trust me. It will be! Have I ever submitted anything less?"

"Ha! I can't argue with that! I've gotta run. Talk with you later?"

"Sure."

It felt good to talk with Hunter like an old friend again. Chey sighed, let her head fall back against the couch and allowed the sadness envelop her. She had fallen for Hunter, even in the distance. She'd come to love living in New York. Too bad she was about to lose both.

The lyrics to a gospel song that her mother often sang about encouraging yourself popped into her head. Chey had come a long way in the past year, blasting through challenges that she'd never imagined before. She'd gotten up the courage to walk away from a bad relationship, move to a new city, go back to school, ace her classes and almost finish a book she'd wanted to write for years. Chey was a new woman—one who accepted and faced challenges fearlessly. She wasn't going to lie down and become a victim to her circumstances now. New York was where she wanted to be and somehow she was going to find a way to stay.

Marching to her room, Chey retrieved her laptop and headed back to the living room. For the next few hours, she finished her final projects for both Hunter's class and her chemistry lab. Then she applied online for more jobs. Her target was Estelle London—the company she dreamed of working for—but there were others. Chey visited the websites of all the cosmetics companies in the city—large and small—and submitted applications. She then reached out to recruiters to help her in the process. By the time she was done, she had several appointments set up with recruiters who specialized in her industry. If she ended up having to go back home to Virginia, at least she could say that she'd done all she could to make her dream work. The moon had taken over for the sun by the time she was finished. The next morning she was going to find a church to attend, take her plan to the altar and ask God to help her make it happen.

Between her savings getting low and her part-time job

not paying enough, she would need to land a higher-paying job by June in order to stay. Then she wouldn't have to say goodbye to New York or to Hunter.

Chapter 29

Today was the day. Hunter left work early to head to the university for his review with the department. The semester had officially ended the day before and he had already posted his students' grades online. He smiled at the thought of how proud he was to give Chey a well-earned A. She had done an exemplary job on her examination of how intellectual property can affect a corporation and its employees. Hunter also knew that she was personally invested in the project because of her desire to create products for an industry giant such as Estelle London.

As good as that made him feel, he couldn't shake the anxiety that cloaked him as he thought about his upcoming meeting. Hunter reached the university with plenty of time to spare so he could settle down before the review. Dipping into the coffee shop right outside the campus grounds, Hunter ordered a medium black coffee, sat in one of the comfortable chairs and perused emails on his cell phone.

"Hello, Professor Barrington." At the sound of her voice, his body awakened. He looked up and Chey was standing in front of him, holding a small cup, looking as if she'd just stepped off the runway of the natural-beauty fashion show. Her style had become a little edgier since she'd been in New York. She now looked sexier than ever in jeans that accentuated her beautiful curves, a fitted T that said I Woke Up Like This and a leather jacket. Her smile was by far her most attractive accessory.

"Hello, Ms. Rodgers." Remembering what it felt like to hold her in his arms, Hunter wanted to reach out and touch her. It took superhuman restraint to sit there and only caress her with his eyes. "What brings you here on a Friday afternoon? Classes are over."

"I have a meeting with my lab professor. He's offered to provide me with more insight on some industry trends that would be helpful in my job search."

Excitement lurched in Hunter's chest. "You're staying in New York?" Hunter hoped he didn't cramp his cool with the eager way that question came out.

"If I land a job or that opportunity with Estelle London. I've been applying everywhere and trying to stay encouraged."

Hunter looked at his watch. "What time is your meeting?"

"I'm early. I wanted to sit and chill for a while before meeting up with him. I really love this coffeehouse. During the semester, I did my homework here all of the time."

Hunter pulled a chair over so she could sit. Chey placed her cup on the bistro table in front of them.

"What are you doing here?" she asked.

"Today is my review."

Chey's mouth formed an O. "That's right! Good luck! How do you feel about it?"

"Good, but you never know. I did my best this semester. I tried to give my students my all and make the work as close to the real world as possible. Hopefully, my effort will speak for itself."

As those words left his mouth, Hunter felt another presence and looked up into the eyes of Kenya. It was obvious that she wasn't happy to see him there with Chey, but what could she say? They'd hardly spoken since their last discussion. Kenya looked away without speaking, lifting her chin slightly higher. Hunter turned and continued his conversation. Once they were done with their coffee, they walked back to campus together.

As they were about to go in separate directions, Chey stopped. "Good luck, Hunter." She straightened his tie and fixed his collar. Hunter lifted his chin to allow room for the adjustment.

Hunter could imagine her doing that to him every morning before he left for work. Suddenly, living alone seemed like a desolate existence. Chey's presence would add zest to his life.

"Thanks. Am I all good now?" he teased, referring to her adjusting his tie.

Chey stepped back. "Let me see." Her eyes washed over him from head to toe. She pulled on his lapel. He stood taller. "I think you're ready." Her brilliant smile flashed and stirred something inside him.

"Thanks again." They gazed at each other for another moment. Hunter focused in on her lips. He knew they wanted to be kissed. He wanted to kiss them. "See you at graduation." He pulled himself out of her world.

"Okay." Chey started toward the science hall.

"Don't forget you promised me a date," Hunter called after her.

"Yeah, yeah. I know."

Hunter watched her make the trek across the grass. It was time for his meeting. Hunter arrived at the conference room to find several individuals, including Martin and Kenya. It had never dawned on him that this would happen in front of a full review board.

"Good afternoon, Hunter." Martin stepped up and shook his hand.

"Good afternoon, Martin." Hunter followed his informal lead before addressing the rest of the individuals. The group consisted of the second in command right under Martin, Ed, someone from HR, another colleague and Kenya.

Martin gestured for Hunter to sit on the opposite end of the table facing the group before taking his seat in the center. A large pile of files sat before him. Hunter felt as though he'd entered into an interrogation. Clearing his throat, he sat erect.

"I'd like to start off by saying how grateful I am to have had the opportunity to teach at Dunford University this past semester. If I am selected to continue my work here, I will be sure to represent the university with dignity and integrity while giving the students my all."

"We appreciate that, Hunter," Martin replied. "Let's get started."

Martin began with a thorough introduction of everyone in attendance and stated each reviewer's purpose for being there. Then he explained the process, which entailed regular interview questions and a review of the statement of purpose they'd asked Hunter to complete regarding his desire for working at the university.

The board kept the questions coming, with everyone asking several. Kenya kept a professional demeanor during the entire process. They moved on to a review of Hunter's curriculum and syllabus and then shared their examination of the students' assignments, which they had asked Hunter to submit prior to the meeting. This part was also arduous, but Hunter understood the intent. They wanted to make sure he graded students justly and showed no favoritism.

After a short break, they reassembled and continued to share their findings on the students' work, its relevance to the real world and Hunter's grading system. Then they took another short break. By now Hunter had loosened his tie and opened the top button of his shirt. He assumed that he was the only person who felt that the room was stuffy.

Finally, the board presented Hunter with an official offer letter for the position of assistant professor outlining salary and benefits. They asked Hunter if he needed time to review the offer. He informed them that he would have their signed copy on Martin's desk by Monday morning. Hunter shook hands and accepted congratulations from his new coworkers.

"The next thing we need to do is get you on the board," Ed said as he patted Hunter's shoulder. "Welcome to the staff."

Kenya was the last to approach Hunter as the room cleared. Taking his hand, she grinned. "You are certainly a man of dignity and integrity, Hunter. Welcome to Dunford University. I hope we can work on being friends again." They shook and Kenya headed out the door.

Hunter felt as if he'd just come up for air. This was finally over. It felt great to achieve something he'd sought for so long. On his way home, he called Blake to share his good fortune and ask if he'd heard anything back from his friend who worked for Estelle London. Unfortunately, Blake hadn't heard anything and they agreed to meet up later for drinks to celebrate.

Now all Hunter had to do was wait for Chey to officially graduate. Once she was no longer a student at Dunford, they were free to pursue one another. Hunter had made plans for an official first date that he hoped Chey would never forget.

Chapter 30

This was a day that Chey had dreamed about for years. Between her and her parents, she didn't know who was more swollen with pride. Her dad, Ray, couldn't stop smiling. Her mother constantly fussed with the dress Chey wore as if she were ten. Deanna wouldn't stop hugging her. She wanted to be completely swept up in the excitement but couldn't help feeling a little down about the fact that she still hadn't landed a job.

The day before, Chey had showed them as much of New York as she could before sending her parents off to dinner and their first Broadway show ever, while she and her sister hung out over at Chelsea Piers. She'd saved and planned to give her parents this experience ever since Hunter mentioned Broadway months ago. Her graduation would be their grand finale before they all headed home. When they were gone, Chey intended to spend the weekend packing items in her apartment that she didn't use frequently. She didn't want to be overwhelmed with packing everything at once. Regardless of how things turned out, Chey wanted to at least be prepared.

Even though Chey had to be at graduation early, her

parents and sister had left with her, deciding to tour the campus and take in local sights. The graduation was taking place inside the athletic center.

Chey joined her classmates. By the time she reached their sitting area, tears were streaming down Chey's smiling face. This had been a long time coming and it felt amazing. She set aside all anxiety about moving back home and relished the moment. Going home didn't mean she couldn't continue to seek jobs in New York. She could always come up for interviews and move back once she landed something. That was exactly what she would do.

Music blossomed through the center while administrators and dignitaries flowed to the stage. The commencement was long, but Chey didn't mind. She couldn't see them but wondered how many times her dad snoozed and had been jabbed in the ribs by her mother. Finally, the time came to call the graduates. Chey took a deep breath. Her cheeks stung from smiling so long and hard, but she continued to smile all the way across the stage. She heard Deanna yell when her name was called. She was called up again to receive an award for graduating with top honors. Chey was certain that the piercing whistle came from her father. She laughed and cried at the same time.

When it was over, Deanna made her take dozens of selfies outside the building, some with the two of them and some with her parents. They could never get her father to look right into the lens. He couldn't understand why they couldn't just take pictures the old-fashioned way.

Deanna poked Chey and tilted her head. Her heart lurched when she saw Hunter walking her way.

"Hey, Hunter." Deanna greeted him first.

"Good to see you, Deanna." Hunter embraced her. "Hello. You must be Mr. and Mrs. Rodgers."

"Yes, son, we are." Ray gave him a firm shake.

"Hello, there—"

Chey interrupted her mother. "Mom, Dad, this is my professor and friend, Hunter Barrington."

"Oh!" Patricia nodded knowingly. Ray looked him up and down.

"I just wanted to say congratulations." Hunter took Chey into a respectable, friendly embrace.

"Thanks!" Chey noted how good he smelled.

"It was a pleasure to meet you, Mr. and Mrs. Rodgers. Deanna, it was good seeing you again." With that, Hunter turned back to Chey. "I'll wait to hear from you. I've made a reservation. Call me once you've seen your family off."

"Will do! See you later."

When Hunter walked off, Patricia cast Chey a sideways glance. "Nice-looking *friend*!"

Chey smiled and rolled her eyes. "Don't start, Mom!"

Ray shook his head and then took Chey by the hand. "Sweetheart. We were a bit nervous about your decision to move here, but we didn't want to stand in the way of your dreams. I just want to let you know that I'm proud of the woman that you've become."

Chey's smile resembled a frown as she fought the urge to tear up. Her heart was filled as she took in her father's words. Patricia hugged her, punctuating her agreement with what her husband had said.

"I'm so proud of you, honey," she said, blinking back tears of her own.

Chey took her family for a quick casual bite to eat before heading over to their hotel to retrieve their bags from storage. When they were safely en route to Virginia, Chey returned home, showered and slipped on a blue knee-length strapless dress as she awaited Hunter's arrival.

Chey's phone rang and she hesitated to answer when she didn't recognize the number.

"Hello."

"I'm looking for Chey Rodgers."

"This is Chey Rodgers. Who's calling, please?"

"This is Elizabeth Graziano calling from Estelle London Incorporated."

Chey froze. She cleared her throat. "Hello, Ms. Graziano. How can I help you?"

She smiled as she spoke to deflect how nervous she was.

"We received your application and samples for the paid apprenticeship program and I would like to schedule an interview with you."

Samples? I didn't send any samples. "That's wonderful. You said samples?"

"Yes. The, uh…" the woman paused as she recalled the names "…Revivify skin cream and Blossom Rose lotion. Those are yours, right?"

They certainly were hers. The lotion had been named after her grandmother Blossom. Revivify was the name she'd given to her rejuvenating skin cream, but how had she gotten ahold of those? Chey certainly hadn't shipped them. They had to have come from the shop, but her parents hadn't said anything about anyone placing an order. She figured they would have mentioned it since they didn't ship to New York often, if at all.

"Yes, ma'am. Those are my products."

"Well, wonderful! When can you come in for an interview? I'll be honest—at this point, we're just looking to go through the motions. We were quite impressed with your product."

Chey wanted to scream. "Does Monday work?" She found herself walking circles in the floor.

"Can you be here at nine thirty?"

"I sure can."

"Okay. Let me give you the address."

"No need, Ms. Graziano. I know exactly where you're located."

"Okay, then. We will meet on the thirtieth floor! I look forward to meeting you Monday, Ms. Rodgers."

When the call ended, Chey jumped up and down. Her dream was unfolding right before her eyes. When she finished her celebratory dance and shout, she wondered how her products had gotten into Ms. Graziano's hands. She dialed her parents. There was no answer. She dialed Deanna. Still no answer. She assumed they were in an area with poor reception as they traveled home. She'd call them back later.

There was a knock on the door. Someone must have let Hunter in the building. Chey blushed at his dreamy gaze when she opened the door. His eyes ate her up as if she were a piece of pie. Without even saying hello, he pulled her into his arms and covered her mouth until she was left breathless. The air even felt lighter after his kiss. Hunter swooped down on her neck and kissed that, too, making Chey squirm with delight.

"We haven't even started our date yet," she teased.

"I couldn't help myself. I wanted to do that for months!" Hunter stepped back and assessed her again. He shook his head, gnawing on his bottom lip. "You look amazing!"

Chey blushed. "Thank you." Hunter didn't look so bad himself in a blue pin-striped suit, ivory shirt and stylish tie.

Hunter took her by the hand. "Are you ready?"

"For what?"

"To try new things."

"Oh, yeah. Where are we going, again?" Chey acted as if she'd forgotten.

Hunter looked at her sideways. "I never mentioned where we were going."

"Oh!" Chey snickered. "I guess that didn't work."

"You of all people should know that I'm great at keeping secrets." A naughty glint flashed in his eyes. Chey laughed. Hunter swallowed her laugh with another kiss. Pulling away, he rested his forehead against hers while they caught their breath. "I can't help myself."

"Don't try to." Chey was still breathless. This time she drew his lips to hers.

"If we keep this up, we'll never go on our date." Hunter's stiffness pressed against her lower stomach.

Chey looked down and giggled. "Maybe we should go now."

Hunter groaned. "Yes. We should."

Downstairs, Hunter had a car waiting to take them to an early dinner cruise. Chey was in awe of the beautiful view of New York and New Jersey along the Hudson as they ate. They took to the floor and danced until Chey's stilettos started giving the balls of her feet grief. To her surprise, Hunter was an incredible dancer. His sexy moves reminded her of his skills in bed and had her swooning by the time the cruise was over.

Chey thought their date was over and was more than ready to go back to her apartment for an after-dinner drink. When the driver continued past several turns that would have taken them back to her neighborhood, she asked Hunter where they were going.

The car pulled up in front of a theater in the heart of Times Square. Chey tapped her feet excitedly as the driver rounded the car and opened the door to help them out.

"Welcome to your first Broadway show, sweetheart!"

Chey threw her arms around Hunter's neck and squeezed tight. Then she held his face in her hands and planted kisses all over him.

"This has been the most amazing day. It's almost overwhelming." Chey wiped the tears that escaped. She'd sacrificed to send her parents to the show the day before, not knowing when or if she'd ever get the opportunity to go herself. Now Hunter was making it happen for her. She hugged him one more time. Hunter took her by the hand.

"I'm glad that I could be a part of it."

Just as they started for the theater, her phone rang.

"Mom! I tried to call you."

"Chey?"

"Yes. I tried to call you."

"Honey, what's all that noise?"

"Oh. I'm out in Times Square." Chey held her hand over her mouth and the receiver. "I was saying that I tried to call you."

"We all fell asleep. I can hardly hear you."

"I'll call you back when I get home tonight."

"Huh? You'll call back?"

"Yes, Ma. I wanted to ask about an order. Love you!"

"Okay."

Chey would have to handle that later. Right now she was getting ready to see her first Broadway show with a man who'd hijacked her heart. She looked up to see which show they were seeing and decided that it didn't even matter. She held Hunter tight as they entered the theater.

When the show was over, she was still in awe. Chey had wept during a few scenes, having no idea that she would be so affected. Their car was waiting outside the theater. On the way home, she invited Hunter up for a cocktail. All she had was one bottle of wine, but that would have to do because she wasn't ready for him to leave.

Inside her apartment, she poured two glasses of cabernet and joined Hunter on the couch.

"Today was…" she shook her head "…unbelievable."

"Did you enjoy the show?"

"Didn't you see me crying an ocean? You have to ask?"

Chey laughed and sipped as she reminisced about the day. "Oh! I forgot to tell you. I got the job!"

"You did!" Hunter leaned forward.

"Well, not officially. I have to go in for an interview on Monday, but the lady said that it's just to go through the motions. The crazy thing is that she said they were impressed with the products that I sent in but I hadn't sent anything to them. I have to find out how they got my stuff."

"So does that mean you're staying in New York?"

"I'm staying!" Chey held up her glass and Hunter touched his against hers in a toast. "So much happened today—graduation, the new job, the dinner cruise, my first Broadway show. Whew! This was the best."

"My lady is worthy of the best."

"Wait! I'm your lady now?" Chey tossed him a narrowed sideways glare.

"You have a problem with that?"

Chey pretended to ponder his question. "Hmm. I guess not."

"I've waited a long time for this, but to make you feel better about it, let's make it official. Chey Rodgers, will you be my lady?"

"Yes, Professor Barrington. I'll be your lady!"

Hunter took her face in his hands and kissed her deeply. Without disconnecting, Chey straddled him, nibbling his lips. Their hands roamed each other's bodies urgently. They paused long enough to appreciate the hunger in each other's eyes. Hunter reached around to her back and unzipped her dress. She squirmed free of it, as well as her bra and matching lace panties.

Chey continued kissing Hunter and she freed him of his clothes. Forfeiting the delight of foreplay, he rolled a condom over his erection, lifted her up and sat her down on top of him. Her head snapped back as he filled her. She rode him. Hunter flicked at her nipples with his tongue. Soon the friction became too delicious for Chey to stand any longer. The walls of her cavern squeezed, suctioning his erection. Chey bucked. Hunter growled. He held her hips, pulling her down harder and faster. She quivered— no longer able to control the shuddering of her muscles. He lifted her off just as his pleasure shot from him, bending his back into a rigid arc. His body folded and released repeatedly until he was finally able to catch his breath.

They started round two by taking turns tasting each other and then satisfying each other's hunger. When they were spent, she lay in his arms until their breathing became steady—his chest to her back, rising and falling as they gave in to the lure of a peaceful slumber.

Chey heard him say, "Finally." She smiled and closed her eyes.

Chapter 31

Hunter quietly removed his clothes, tiptoed into the bathroom and snatched the shower curtain back. Chey's screams pierced his ears and he laughed.

"That's not funny!" She pouted with her hand over her heart. Hunter leaned over into the stream of water and kissed her pouting lips. "I didn't even hear you come up the stairs."

"How can you hear anything with this music blasting?" He motioned toward her phone resting on the countertop.

"That's my get-up-and-go playlist. It gets me going in the morning!" She chuckled, rinsing the lather from her body.

Hunter suddenly felt hot water splash on him. He ducked. "What was that for?"

"I found out how Estelle London got my products. I spoke to my dad and he said the only order that he shipped to New York went to a company named Barrington and Associates." Hunter remained quiet. "Mm-hmm! Nothing to say, huh?"

"You're welcome?" Hunter roared, happy his meddling had worked for the best. Fortunately, she didn't seem upset.

"How long will it be before you're ready to go?" Hunter said, reaching for his toothbrush.

"Just give me about twenty minutes."

"Yeah, right," he said under his breath before brushing.

"I heard that!" Chey pushed the curtain aside and peered at him. "Are you getting in?"

"Mm-hmm." Hunter bobbed his head to her music as he brushed his teeth. "I'm all sticky from helping my parents set up the backyard for the barbecue," he said after rinsing his mouth.

Hunter joined her in the shower, and because Chey had been hard to resist since the first day he laid eyes on her, an erection swelled at the sight of her slick naked body. He palmed her breasts from behind.

"Hunter! I've already washed."

Pressing his body against hers, he kissed the back of her neck and behind her ears, muting her protests. Chey turned around, lifted onto her toes and met his lips as the water rained down on them.

"We…have…to…go," she said between kisses.

"Then let's make this quick."

"You're so bad." She giggled.

Hunter disappeared into the bedroom and returned with a condom. He lifted her. Chey wrapped her legs around his waist and he entered her slickness. After a while, she slid her feet back to the shower floor, turned and bent over. Hunter eased into her from behind, held her by the hips and thrust until his release made his legs too weak to stand on, but he didn't stop until she met her release and crooned his name. They washed each other and exited the shower.

In his room, they dressed—Chey in a short floral sundress and Hunter in jeans and a designer T-shirt.

"Is that what you're wearing?"

Chey looked down at her attire. "Yes. Why?"

"I planned on taking the bike."

"Oh. You hadn't told me. I'll change." Chey dug in her overnight bag and pulled out jeans and a beaded tank. Hunter loved that she had taken a liking to his motorcycles.

"I need to make room for you to put some of your stuff here."

"Is that an invitation?" Chey raised a brow.

"Who knows?" Hunter walked out of the room, letting his ambiguous response hang in the air. "Come on, lady. Let's go," he said, briefly peeking his head back in. He huffed at Chey in the mirror combing her hair.

"Had you let me shower in peace, I'd be ready by now."

Hunter glanced into the room once again, wearing a silly smile. Down on the first level of his four-floor brownstone, Hunter pulled out a light riding jacket and helmets.

They had been inseparable since her graduation in mid-May, but today would be her first time meeting his parents face-to-face. He'd accompanied her to Virginia for Memorial Day weekend, and each weekend since then, they'd explored different areas in Brooklyn. Hunter made it his duty to make her fall in love with his borough the way she'd fallen in love with Manhattan. He hoped that she would be convinced enough to move there when her lease was up in October.

Chey came strolling down Hunter's steps as if she belonged there. Hunter handed her the light jacket he'd bought for when they went riding and a helmet that matched his. They mounted his Ducati and headed to his parents' home in Long Island for their annual Fourth of July party.

Naturally, holiday traffic was atrocious and it took double the usual amount of time to get there. When they finally arrived, his hands were numb from the bike's vibration.

"Are you nervous?" Hunter asked, helping her out of her helmet.

"Of course." Chey adjusted her jeans, which had ridden up her leg.

"Don't be." Hunter pecked her lips. "My parents are some of the coolest people on this side of the Mason–Dixon Line." He took her by the hand and led her to the backyard.

"Drew's here," he acknowledged, inclining his head toward his brother's motorcycle.

Music and laughter met them as they drew closer to the backyard. Hunter could hear splashing from the kids in the pool. Adrenaline surged as he prepared to introduce Chey to his parents.

He pushed open the gate with authority and yelled, "Hey! What's with all the noise back here?"

At first people paused, then laughed as they realized it was Hunter.

"Hey, man. What's good?" his uncle said and hugged him before assessing Chey approvingly over the top of his glasses. "Who's your friend, young man?"

Hunter introduced them. Yelling erupted at some commotion near the grill. Hunter looked over to see his mom and dad in the midst of their usual antics, dancing—this time doing the bump while the crowd cheered them on.

"See." Hunter pulled Chey to him. "I told you they were cool."

When they finished their routine, Hunter presented Chey to them. Floyd shook her hand. Joyce pulled her into a tight embrace, shifted her back to arm's length and looked her over.

"Oh! She's a pretty one, Floyd. Isn't she?" Her smile was warm.

"Thank you, ma'am." Chey smiled back.

"Wow! And she says '*ma'am*.' Good ole Southern manners. You're welcome, baby. Make yourself at home and enjoy the party." Joyce let her go and craned her neck in her son's direction. "Hunter, get the lady something to eat."

"Will do, Mom."

Joyce went to walk away and turned back. "Wait. You can have babies, can't you?"

Chey's mouth fell open.

"Mom!"

"Now, Joyce!" Floyd chided.

Joyce's hearty laugh made everyone within earshot laugh. "I'm just messing with you." Her expression turned serious and she looked over her glasses. "But you can, can't you?"

"Mom!"

"Alright. Alright!" Joyce laughed all the way back to the house.

Blake, Cadence, Drew and Alana came out and greeted Chey. Then Cadence and Alana took her to the gazebo to do what girls did. Hunter wasn't quite sure what that was but saw that she was comfortable, so he let her be.

For the next few hours, Chey seemed to enjoy herself in the girls' company, while the brothers mingled with family and friends. Kids swam, music flowed, people danced and everyone ate.

Floyd banged on the table, garnering everyone's attention. "I want to make an announcement." He waved his wife over and put his arm around her. Staring at her lovingly for a brief moment, he cleared his throat. "This wonderful woman—" he looked at her again "—my amazing wife, is being honored by her sorority for her many years of community service and her selfless contributions to the lives of underprivileged women and girls. I, for one, am extremely proud of her and I'm glad to see that she is being recognized for all the wonderful work she does." Joyce beamed as Floyd leaned over and kissed her forehead.

"I'd like to invite you all to the gala, which is next Saturday evening. I'm very excited about this honor and hope many of you can make it. That includes you, too, Chey," Joyce said.

Chey smiled sheepishly and nodded. "Thank you so much for the invitation, Mrs. Barrington, and congratulations."

Hunter sidled up behind her, wrapping his arm around her waist. "I guess we've got a gala to attend."

"But I don't have a dress." Chey looked genuinely concerned.

"Don't worry about the details. I'll take care of those." Hunter fulfilled that promise. Before they left the barbecue, he asked for Cadence and Alana's assistance.

The next week, Chey met up with the girls and went shopping. Hunter had no idea what she would look like when he pulled up in front of her building in his convertible, the car he saved for special occasions. He took the steps two at a time, anxious to see his lady.

When Chey opened the door, the air left Hunter's lungs in a rush. Several moments passed as he stared. She spun around, giving a three-dimensional view of her form-hugging red halter gown and silver shoes. Hunter always thought she was beautiful, but tonight she looked exceptionally stunning.

Lifting his chin, Chey closed his mouth. "A bug is going to fly in there." She pecked his lips. His arms slid around her back and he pulled her tighter.

Pulling back, he rested his forehead against hers—something that had become a familiar gesture between them. "I think I'm in love."

Chey swatted him, laughing and shaking her head.

"Silly! I guess that means you like what you see." Chey twisted from side to side, presenting her ensemble and relishing in the compliment.

"No. That means I really think I'm in love."

Chey's smile vanished. She looked at the serious expression on Hunter's face. He nodded. Now her mouth hung open.

"I love you, Chey."

Impulsively, she covered her mouth with a shaking hand. "Oh my goodness, Hunter. I love you, too."

They collapsed into each other's arms and stayed there for a while before sealing their love with another kiss.

Taking her by the hand, Hunter led her down the steps. He truly felt like a prince. Gently, he placed her in the car as if she were a delicate doll and sauntered to the driver's side. They held hands all the way to the gala and remained devoted to each other's sides throughout all the festivities. No one seemed to be there but them.

When the event was over, they cruised with the top down, enjoying the breeze. Hunter took her to a park along the west side of Upper Manhattan. First they got out, walked and talked for a little while, taking in the scenery and the lights at night. They went back to the car and, instead of getting in, sat on the hood, letting the moon cast its treasured light over their newfound love.

Hunter put his forehead against hers and said, "You're mine now!"

"Finally," Chey said and lifted her lips to his.

* * * * *

Love creates its own rules

Bridget Anderson

Ascending the corporate ladder has consumed most of Tayler Carter's adult life. Now the savvy VP is ready for a well-deserved retreat. A B and B in rural Kentucky is the perfect change of pace. But her host is no unsophisticated farm boy. Rugged hunk Rollin Coleman is educating Tayler in the wonders of natural food and down-home passion. Can he count on Tayler to leave her fast-paced world behind and together create a place they can both call home?

COLEMAN HOUSE

Available May 2016!

HARLEQUIN®
www.Harlequin.com

KPBA4490516

Second-chance romance

AlTonya Washington

KIMANI™ ROMANCE

Provocative
ATTRACTION

AlTonya Washington

Provocative
ATTRACTION

Viva Hail always dreamed of a world far away from her Philadelphia roots, and it cost her the man she loved. Now Rook Lourdess is back in her life. As her personal bodyguard, the world-renowned security expert sweeps her off to his chalet in Italy, rekindling a desire that could forgive the mistakes of the past. Will their reignited passion offer a chance to write a new ending, or is Rook giving in to a temptation that could break his heart once again?

"Filled with passion and emotional sizzle."
—*RT Book Reviews* on *HIS TEXAS TOUCH*

Available May 2016!

REQUEST YOUR FREE BOOKS!

2 FREE NOVELS
PLUS 2 FREE GIFTS!

KIMANI™
ROMANCE

Love's ultimate destination!

YES! Please send me 2 FREE Harlequin® Kimani™ Romance novels and my 2 FREE gifts (gifts are worth about $10). After receiving them, if I don't wish to receive any more books, I can return the shipping statement marked "cancel." If I don't cancel, I will receive 4 brand-new novels every month and be billed just $5.44 per book in the U.S. or $5.99 per book in Canada. That's a savings of at least 16% off the cover price. It's quite a bargain! Shipping and handling is just 50¢ per book in the U.S. and 75¢ per book in Canada.* I understand that accepting the 2 free books and gifts places me under no obligation to buy anything. I can always return a shipment and cancel at any time. Even if I never buy another book, the two free books and gifts are mine to keep forever.

168/368 XDN GH4P

Name _____ (PLEASE PRINT)

Address _____ Apt. #

City _____ State/Prov. _____ Zip/Postal Code

Signature (if under 18, a parent or guardian must sign)

Mail to the **Reader Service:**
IN U.S.A.: P.O. Box 1867, Buffalo, NY 14240-1867
IN CANADA: P.O. Box 609, Fort Erie, Ontario L2A 5X3

Want to try two free books from another line?
Call 1-800-873-8635 or visit www.ReaderService.com.

* Terms and prices subject to change without notice. Prices do not include applicable taxes. Sales tax applicable in N.Y. Canadian residents will be charged applicable taxes. Offer not valid in Quebec. This offer is limited to one order per household. Not valid for current subscribers to Harlequin® Kimani™ Romance books. All orders subject to credit approval. Credit or debit balances in a customer's account(s) may be offset by any other outstanding balance owed by or to the customer. Please allow 4 to 6 weeks for delivery. Offer available while quantities last.

Your Privacy—The Reader Service is committed to protecting your privacy. Our Privacy Policy is available online at www.ReaderService.com or upon request from the Reader Service.

We make a portion of our mailing list available to reputable third parties that offer products we believe may interest you. If you prefer that we not exchange your name with third parties, or if you wish to clarify or modify your communication preferences, please visit us at www.ReaderService.com/consumerchoice or write to us at Reader Service Preference Service, P.O. Box 9062, Buffalo, NY 14240-9062. Include your complete name and address.

KROM15

SPECIAL EXCERPT FROM

⊕ HARLEQUIN®

Mariah Drayson is set to run the Seattle branch of her family's legendary patisserie. And when she and high-end coffee importer Everett Myers join forces, he knows they're a winning team. But is Mariah prepared to reveal the secret that could cost her a future with Everett?

Read on for a sneak peek at
CAPPUCCINO KISSES, the first exciting installment of Harlequin Kimani Romance's continuity,
THE DRAYSONS: SPRINKLED WITH LOVE!

"Everett." She swallowed the lump that suddenly formed by having the businessman yet again in her crosshairs.

"Hey." He smiled, showing off his sparkling white teeth.

"Hi." Mariah didn't know why she couldn't think of anything but a one-syllable word, and her heart was hammering in her chest.

"Surprised to see me?"

"Actually, no, I'm not," she replied, finding her voice. "You've been persistent, so I doubted today would be any different."

"Is that why you dressed up for me today?" Everett asked, raking every inch of her figure with his magnetic gaze.

Mariah started to say no, but knew it would be a bold-faced lie, so she led with the truth. "What if I did?"

Everett's eyes darkened and his expression shifted from flirtatious to something different, something she didn't recognize but knew to be dangerous. "Come from behind the counter and I'll show you."

Mariah wasn't sure she wanted to leave the safety that the counter provided. Everett looked as if he was ready to pounce and she wasn't certain she could or would fight him off.

"Mariah." He said her name again and it sounded silky and seductive coming from his lips.

She instinctively obeyed, ignoring the warning signals going off in her brain to beware. When she rounded the corner of the counter, Everett captured her hand and brought her forward until she was inches from his face, from his lips. Sensuously full lips that she had a hard time not focusing on.

"I'm glad you've come around to seeing things my way," he said, as his large hands skimmed over her forearms.

"Did I have much choice?"

He chuckled. "No, I didn't plan on giving up. But I have to admit that I didn't come here solely to see you."

"No?" She tried not to appear offended by the comment.

"Don't look so crestfallen," he said, caressing her chin with the pad of his thumb. "I have a business offer for you."

Why did he have to keep touching her? It was scrambling her brain and she couldn't think straight. "B-business? What business would you and I have?"

Don't miss CAPPUCCINO KISSES
by Yahrah St. John, available June 2016
wherever Harlequin® Kimani Romance™
books and ebooks are sold.